MONSIEUR PAMPLEMOUSSE AND THE TANGLED WEB

Monsieur Pamplemousse and his trusty dog, Pommes Frites are called into Le Guide's offices early one morning and presented with a string of Leclerq's plaintive conundrums – all relating to his mobster uncle-in-law. These include a letter about a juicy steak turned brisket, a dead restaurant owner, a giant truffle delivered by post and the imminent arrival of the vivacious Caterina to the Gare des Lyons. All of which Pamplemousse has been called upon to help.

MONSIEUR PAMPLEMOUSSE
AND THE TANGLED WEB

Monsieur Pamplemousse and the Tangled Web

by

Michael Bond

Magna Large Print Books
Long Preston, North Yorkshire,
BD23 4ND, England.

British Library Cataloguing in Publication Data.

Bond, Michael
    Monsieur Pamplemousse and the tangled web.

    A catalogue record of this book is
    available from the British Library

    ISBN   978-0-7505-4109-1

First published in Great Britain by Allison & Busby Ltd. in 2014

Copyright © 2014 by Michael Bond

Cover illustration by arrangement with Allison & Busby Ltd.

The moral right of the author is hereby asserted in accordance
with the Copyright, Designs and Patents Act, 1988

Published in Large Print 2015 by arrangement with
Allison & Busby Ltd.

Magna Large Print is an imprint of Library Magna Books Ltd.

Printed and bound in Great Britain by
T.J. (International) Ltd., Cornwall, PL28 8RW

'Oh, what a tangled web we weave,
When first we practise to deceive'

SIR WALTER SCOTT
1771–1832

CHAPTER ONE

It all began with a telephone call from the Director of *Le Guide*, France's premier gastronomic bible, summoning him to its headquarters in the 7th *arrondissement* of Paris, ASAP. It wasn't the first time such a thing had happened, and doubtless it wouldn't be the last.

Monsieur Pamplemousse glanced at his watch. It showed a few minutes after 07.30. The only thing he could say for sure about the call was that it was much earlier than usual. It would happen when he was looking forward to a leisurely breakfast.

There were those who would have said that the shameless way in which the Director took advantage of his subordinate's experience of life in the raw during his years with the Paris Sûreté was beyond belief. Foremost was his wife, Doucette.

'I wonder what the old so-and-so wants this time?' she said. 'You haven't been back home after your last assignment for five minutes, let alone had time to readjust.'

Monsieur Pamplemousse didn't rise to the bait. Far from viewing it as being the downside of his work, he secretly welcomed such diversions.

Being a food inspector might sound glamorous to those outside the profession – 'I should be so lucky' summed up most people's view of his work – 'A job made in heaven' was the opinion of those of a more romantic disposition.

And so it could be at times, but there were exceptions, and the month he had just completed in the Aude mountains was a typical case in point. It had rained practically every day, and on two occasions he had genuinely feared for his life when he'd encountered a flash flood.

That apart, there were moments when having to report in minute detail on every morsel of food he had eaten while it was still fresh in his mind, coupled with weeks on the road far from home, could be tedious in the extreme. From that point of view, he didn't know what he would do without Pommes Frites for company.

But there again, the grass was always greener on the other side of the fence. The occasions when he was called on to rescue Monsieur Leclercq from yet another predicament were like manna from heaven; a case of having the best of both worlds.

Helping himself to a second croissant, he carefully broke it in two and reached for the butter dish. 'There is no great hurry,' he said. 'It's a thirty-kilometre drive from his home outside Paris, and if he goes at his normal pace it will probably take him a good hour.'

'I wouldn't bet on it,' said Doucette. 'If you ask me he was phoning from his car. I could hear other traffic in the background. It sounded as though someone was hooting at him. Besides, the message was very short and sharp. He didn't even wait for an answer.'

'No mention of the dreaded word?'

'Estragon?' Doucette shook her head. 'No, thank goodness.'

Monsieur Pamplemousse wiped his mouth clean with a napkin and rose from the table. That put a different complexion on the matter.

Estragon was *Le Guide's* code word for use in an emergency: a major breakdown in their Poulanc DB23 mainframe computer, perhaps. Or, worse still, someone attempting to break into it just when they were in the final stages of preparing the latest edition which, following tradition, was due to be published on the third Tuesday in March.

Monsieur Leclercq often became twitchy as the day drew near, but the fact that he hadn't made use of the vital code word suggested it must be something personal.

'I had better go, Couscous,' he said. 'It could be serious, and I doubt if anyone else is in the office yet.'

Pausing only to kiss Doucette goodbye, Monsieur Pamplemousse slipped on his jacket and a few minutes later, with Pommes Frites at his side, he set off as fast as he could in his *deux chevaux*. Clearly, there was no time to be lost.

The Director had made no mention of his friend and mentor's presence being required. Nevertheless, he automatically took him along in case he might be of assistance.

For once Place Clichy was free of traffic jams. Cutting down the rue de Saint-Pétersbourg towards St Augustin, he weaved his way in and out of the incoming commuter traffic which more than once threatened to block their way in the maze of one-way streets between St Augustin and the Champs Élysées. Heading south, they eventually crossed the Seine in record time via the Pont des Invalides.

Pommes Frites, who had been playing his part as ever, shifting his weight to and fro in the front passenger seat in order to prevent their toppling over on sharp bends, heaved a sigh of relief. Having been deprived of his usual early morning walk, the call of nature was beckoning him in no uncertain terms, but mixed in with it was admiration at his master's prowess in parking the car in the tiniest of gaps without the slightest jolt before he turned off the engine.

Not that there was anything surprising in that. Monsieur Pamplemousse took pride in his parking. Pommes Frites had often heard him talking to his colleagues on the subject. It had to do with the designers of the car making sure there was a wheel at all four corners. It was his proud boast he could turn a 2CV round on an old two-franc piece.

It didn't seem to apply to dogs. Pommes Frites had a leg at all four corners, but he often had trouble fitting himself onto a rug, let alone an old coin.

They covered the last hundred or so metres to *Le Guide's* headquarters in the rue Fabert on foot.

Seeing the large old oak double doors outside the main entrance were still firmly closed, Monsieur Pamplemousse reached inside an inner pocket of his jacket for a plastic card embossed with *Le Guide's* motif:

two *escargots* rampant. Holding it against a brass plate let into the stone wall to their right, he waited patiently while a small door let into the nearest main one slowly opened to afford entry.

There was no sign of life in the hut just inside the main entrance. Old Rambaud, the gatekeeper, couldn't have arrived yet. Nor was the Director's Citroën DS5 in its usual place outside the private entrance to his suite on the seventh floor.

Pausing by the artificial pool, which was the central feature of a vast courtyard, he waited a moment or two while Pommes Frites, having first slaked his thirst, balanced himself on three legs in order to focus his attention on other urgent matters brought on by the journey. Normally it would have been made ten times worse by the close proximity of a fountain, but for once the pool lay empty and the fountain was silent.

Deprived momentarily of one of life's illicit pleasures he changed his mind and on second thoughts, disappeared into some shrubbery outside the main entrance to the building.

A few moments later, following on behind, Monsieur Pamplemousse glanced over his shoulder as he mounted the steps. It was a

16

good thing Rambaud hadn't been around. He was grumpy enough at the best of times. A man of few words, most of which didn't bear repeating, he would have exhausted his vocabulary had he witnessed Pommes Frites' behaviour.

The long reception desk was also un-manned, but the very fact of their gaining admittance at all suggested the night porter must be doing his rounds. Somewhere in the distance he could hear a bell ringing.

Signalling Pommes Frites to follow him, he led the way across the hall towards a bank of self-operated lifts.

Entering one that was standing idle, its doors open at the ready, he noted the floor indicator above the one next to it registered seven. Either the Director's secretary, Véron-ique, had come in early as well, or the Director had beaten them both to it. If that were the case he must have parked some-where outside, probably in the vast under-ground car park beneath the Esplanade des Invalides. Doubtless one of its employees was counting his good fortune having pocketed a handsome tip for keeping an eye on it.

He didn't have long to wait for an answer. As they reached the seventh floor and the lift doors slid open, a familiar voice rang out. 'At last, Pamplemousse,' called Monsieur Leclercq. 'I was beginning to wonder what was keeping you.

'You are forgetting something,' he added as they approached his office via an open door outside Véronique's office on the far side of the corridor.

'I am?' repeated Monsieur Pamplemousse. He signalled Pommes to halt and began feeling in his pockets.

'I am referring to today's password,' said the Director testily. 'How do I know you are who you say you are?'

Monsieur Pamplemousse reached down to a trouser leg. 'I have a mole on my left knee,' he said. 'It is listed on my P47 form of personal details.'

Monsieur Leclercq affected a shudder. 'I have no wish to see your left knee, Pamplemousse,' he boomed. 'I haven't fully digested my breakfast as yet.'

'I could hardly be anybody else,' said Monsieur Pamplemousse. 'We came as quickly as we could and I didn't have time to check today's code word via the security line.'

'That isn't good enough, Pamplemousse,' reproved Monsieur Leclercq. 'We happen to be on Red Alert. It seems we may have an intruder in the building. Some hidden sensors

18

in the shrubbery outside the main entrance detected a heavy object. That is why the alarm bells are ringing.

'I will let it pass on this occasion, Aristide, but please be more careful in future.' Waving one hand vaguely in the air to indicate they should make their own seating arrangements, the Director collapsed – there was no other word for it – collapsed with an impressive hiss of escaping air into the armchair behind his desk.

Reflecting that security in *Le Guide's* headquarters during the run-up to publication day must make that at Fort Knox resemble Galeries Lafayette when their mid-summer sales were in full swing, Monsieur Pamplemousse selected a chair nearest to him and placed it in front of the Director's desk.

'How were things in the Aude?' asked Monsieur Leclercq, while his subordinate made himself comfortable. 'Bracing as ever, I imagine.'

'Wet,' said Monsieur Pamplemousse. At least the Director knew where he had been the past few weeks. 'There is no other word for it. It rained nearly every day. They hardly had need for the Canal du Midi connecting the Mediterranean with the Atlantic Ocean.'

His response was of no great moment, for

Monsieur Leclercq immediately launched into what was clearly foremost in his mind. 'Aristide,' he said. 'I am in urgent need of your help.'

Had Pommes Frites been born with a sense of humour, he would have been laughing his head off by now. But there were other, more serious matters on his mind.

Normally, when they were summoned to what was known by others in the building as the 'Holiest of Holies', something tasty would be laid out on a mat to keep him occupied. Nothing too grand, of course. Monsieur Leclercq disliked the sound of bones being chewed, so a choice titbit of something soft and easily disposed of was usually the order of the day – a slice or two of *pâté de campagne* cut into small squares was one of his favourites – but for once there was nothing. Absolutely nothing!

In fact ... Pommes Frites raised his head and sniffed pointedly ... it was worse than nothing.

His nostrils detected an elusive, but nonetheless inescapable smell of something vaguely familiar in the air. Taste buds began to salivate as he racked his brains trying to think what it could possibly be.

Given that it was hard to tell exactly where

the scent was coming from, he gave up the struggle for the time being, and having turned round and round in a circle several times, settled himself down at his master's feet, luxuriating in the rays of an unusually spring-like February sunshine entering the Director's office via a vast picture window which ran the entire length of the mansard floor on the east side of the building.

Monsieur Pamplemousse, on the other hand, felt sorely tempted to say 'Not for the first time, *Monsieur.*'

However, rather than sully the atmosphere before he knew the true reason for their visit, he resisted the notion and simply inclined his head to acknowledge what was undoubtedly a rare compliment. It showed that deep down Monsieur Leclercq didn't take their presence entirely for granted.

As the seconds ticked away, it struck him rather forcibly they needn't have hurried. The Director must have more than one matter on his mind for despite his apparent urgency in calling the meeting, he seemed to be playing for time; metaphorically sharpening pencils as a means of putting off the evil moment.

Doubtless he was making some last-minute adjustments to his mental agenda as he began sorting various items into some kind of order, rearranging what was already an immaculately tidy desk, much as Véronique must have left it the previous evening.

Eventually, having reached a decision and suddenly aware of the others' discomfort as they sat blinking in the sun's rays, he pressed a button beneath his desk and waited a moment or two while an awning slid silently into place, diffusing the light as it went.

'You may be wondering why I called you in at such short notice, Aristide,' he said, at last.

'We came as soon as we could, *Monsieur,*' replied Monsieur Pamplemousse non-committally. 'Pommes Frites hasn't even had his morning constitutional as yet,' he added pointedly.

That, too, was like water off the proverbial duck's back. The Director brushed the news aside as though it were of no account. 'We all have to take the rough with the smooth, Pamplemousse,' he said brusquely. 'It is hardly the end of the world.'

Monsieur Pamplemousse refrained from saying, 'Try telling that to a dog dying to go out first thing in the morning.'

The very thought of Monsieur Leclercq taking Pommes Frites for an early morning walk struck him as being a bizarre flight of fancy. For a start he couldn't picture him setting out in the Paris streets armed with a plastic bag. Nor could he visualise Madame Leclercq being first in the queue to accompany him. And if she did, her bag would undoubtedly bear the colophon of some well-known couturier in the avenue Montaigne in case they met someone she knew.

The Director suddenly reached a decision. Leaning across the desk, he handed Monsieur Pamplemousse a single sheet of A4 paper. 'Read that, Aristide... It is a *courrier électronique* from a member of the Club des Cent.'

Masking his irritation at the Director's insistence on using the long-winded French term for what was after all a common or garden email, Monsieur Pamplemousse suppressed an inward whistle.

Of all the clubs in the world, the Club des Cent had to be one of the most exclusive and no doubt warranted the distinction. Its strictly male membership was drawn from the cream of French hierarchy in the realms of politics, business, and the law. They met from time to time, not merely to discuss the problems of their various callings, the state of the world in general and France in particular, but not to put too fine a point on it, with the

23

aim of enjoying a good meal together, followed by a long discussion as to its pros and cons compared with those they had partaken of on previous occasions. Wine and liqueurs would figure largely in the ensuing debate, and the net result was a veritable guide to all that was best in French cuisine. The contents of the email were brief and to the point. It seemed that a distant relative of the writer ... a cousin from the United States ... was recently in Paris for a business meeting and during the course of a necessarily brief visit, on the recommendation of one of the club's members, he had dined at an off-the-beaten-track restaurant in the 3rd *arrondissement*. Unfortunately, not speaking French, he went to the wrong address where, purely on the basis of having been shown an example of what had to be the most luscious steak he had ever seen in his life, a glistening *filet de bœuf* fully two inches thick and beautifully marbled, he ordered it there and then.

'Rare,' had been his instructions to the waitress. 'Tell the chef to simply show it to the grill – no more.'

Having been kept waiting a good twenty minutes, during which time he had been plied with drinks, which not only added considerably to his bill, but dulled his taste buds into the bargain, the steak of his dreams had transmogrified into a mangy piece of brisket from an unidentifiable animal. A camel perhaps, or a buffalo that had died of old age, and not before time.

It was a sorry tale, and to make matters worse, as the man stalked out of the restaurant in high dudgeon, he caught sight of his waitress armed with what was obviously the same steak, homing in on some new arrivals before they had time even to sit down. For a brief moment he had felt tempted to go back inside and warn them it probably spent its life attached to the plate by means of a strip of Velcro or some such fiendish device in case anyone took it into their head to give it a tentative poke with a fork before it was returned to the kitchen. But having caught what he took to be the helmsman's menacing eye, he thought better of it.

'Such happenings,' said the writer, 'are not only an embarrassment to one of our members, but they cause irreparable harm to our country in the eyes of visitors from other parts of the world. I realise you are not a member of our club, *Monsieur*, but please, *please* do something about the matter before it is too late...'

'One reason why I am not a member,' explained Monsieur Leclercq, hastily retrieving the email, 'and what makes the Club des Cent so exclusive, is that membership is strictly confined to one hundred names. Only when a member dies can a new one be taken on board. The thing is, what can we do about it?'

'What is a helmsman?' asked Monsieur Pamplemousse, for want of anything better to say on the spur of the moment. 'I cannot picture it being a word which has the approval of the Académie Française.'

'And never will,' said the Director. 'I understand it is an Americanism for the man in charge, and in this instance I gather he looked a bruiser if ever there was one.'

'Ah!' said Monsieur Pamplemousse.

'I understand what the person who wrote the letter is saying,' he continued, 'and the whole thing was undoubtedly a botch-up of monumental proportions, but there are black sheep in every walk of life, and the restaurant world is not without its fair share of them.

'I doubt if the establishment in question aspires to being listed in *Le Guide*, or anywhere else of note for that matter ... rather the reverse. A visit from the Food Fraud Squad and a lecture about the perils of "passing off" will soon set things right. And if it doesn't, then so much the worse for them. They will be leant on in no uncertain manner.

'If you wish, *Monsieur*, I will put the word around in the right quarter. As you may recall, I spent some time with the food squad during my time with the Sûreté. Seeking out run-of-the-mill chicken being sold as birds from Bresse; scales with doctored weights; margarine in croissants instead of butter; that kind of underhand behaviour. But nothing quite so blatantly criminal as the one described in the letter.'

It struck him that if that was all the Director had in mind it could have been left until later in the day.

'I fear that isn't the end of the story,' said Monsieur Leclercq gloomily. 'The moral of which is: if you don't wish matters to be spread far and wide to all and sundry, as far as is humanly possible, keep them away from my wife.

'As ill luck would have it, Chantal happened to be on the phone to her Uncle Rocco shortly after I received the *courrier électronique* you have just read ... *he* phoned *her*, I might add, not the other way round...'

'Uncle Rocco?' broke in Monsieur Pamplemousse. 'The one who has a laundry business in Sicily? As I recall, he is often

27

referred to as Uncle Caputo because of his Mafia connections.'

'Unfortunately, yes, Pamplemousse,' said the Director gloomily. 'And he enjoys the nickname for very good reasons. He has a swift way of dealing with those who cross his path. "Ironing out the creases", is his way of putting it.'

'*Malheur?*' hazarded Monsieur Pamplemousse. 'Bad news?'

'With a capital *M*,' said Monsieur Leclercq. '*Malheureusement!* I sometimes wish with all my heart he would sever his connections with what he calls "my friends in the mob", if only for Chantal's peace of mind, but alas it is not to be.'

'In that respect the rules of the Cosa Nostra bear a certain likeness to the Club des Cent,' said Monsieur Pamplemousse. 'Only in reverse. In the case of the Mafia, once you become a member there is only one way out, I fear. Feet first. And I can't see that happening. As you wisely say, *Monsieur,* your wife's uncle didn't come by the nickname *Caputo* without a very good reason. What is it this time?'

The Director glanced nervously over his shoulder. 'Walls have ears, Aristide,' he said. 'I thought I heard a noise. I cannot stress too highly that Uncle Rocco is not an actual member of the Cosa Nostra. He has no aspirations of becoming a godfather or anything like that. He simply acts as their go-between from time to time.'

'That's his story,' thought Monsieur Pamplemousse. In his experience, one involvement quickly led to another and there was no going back.

'However,' continued the Director, 'to keep up her end of the conversation Chantal told him all about the episode with the steak. She thought he might be interested. People in that walk of life are known to have affinities with the restaurant trade. They often use them as a kind of gathering place.'

'Not always to their advantage,' said Monsieur Pamplemousse. 'Food is very important to Italians and the Mafia is no exception. Like any other body of people they have their favourites. Steakhouses are where they can be often be found *en masse* as it were; hence the number of massacres that have taken place in such places over the years. Sparks Steak House in New York is the most written about example.

'Historically, it took place in New York in 1985, when Paul Castellano, head of the Gambino crime family, was gunned down.

'One could cite many others. It is a part of their code, since it affords the victims enjoyment of their last meal on this earth before they die, although in Paul Castellano's case he didn't even get to do that. It happened just as he was about to enter Sparks.'

'Do you know what Uncle Rocco said about our restaurant?' asked the Director.

Monsieur Pamplemousse shook his head.

'"It isn't on any list that I know of, *bambina*. But don't you worry your pretty little head about it. I will see what can be arranged. That kind of behaviour gives the Mafia a bad name."'

'I will see what I can do...' began Monsieur Pamplemousse.

'I am very much afraid, Pamplemousse,' broke in the Director gloomily, 'it is too late. The so-called helmsman of the restaurant in question met with an unfortunate accident on his way home late one night. His body was found floating in the canal St Martin shortly after the night in question.'

Monsieur Pamplemousse allowed himself a brief whistle. *'Sacrebleu!'* he exclaimed. 'And the restaurant? What has happened to it?'

'Closed for staff holidays,' said the Director. 'Or so I am told.'

'That covers a multitude of sins,' said

30

Monsieur Pamplemousse. 'When did all this happen? I have to confess to being a bit out of date with events in Paris.'

'I don't have an actual date,' said Monsieur Leclercq. 'It must have been hushed up at the time. Probably at the request of the minister responsible for tourism. But I know who did it. Or rather, I can guess who ordered it to be done, and it is rather too near home for my liking.

'It is a travesty of justice, Aristide. What became of the old adage about making the punishment fit the crime? Chantal's uncle has always been very good to her. She is the *pomme* of his eye, but a line has to be drawn somewhere...'

'I'm sure he meant well,' said Monsieur Pamplemousse. 'It is simply a fact of life with the Mafia. They have different priorities to us. Life is cheap in Sicily, but on the whole their quarrels are kept within the various families. Innocent passers-by have little to worry about. I imagine someone just a phone call away must have owed your wife's uncle a favour.

'There would also be an element of punishing the restaurant owner for falling down on his job and allowing the scam to be brought to light. It would have upset Uncle Rocco's

31

sensibilities. He is a very fastidious person in that respect. To use a classic phrase, the owner of the restaurant had it coming to him.'

'Chantal didn't get a wink of sleep all that night thinking about it,' said Monsieur Leclercq. 'I hope it doesn't mean the Mafia are contemplating moving in over here. It would happen when we are in the throes of putting next year's guide to bed. It could wreak havoc with some of our entries. Things are difficult enough as it is with all these iPhones and iPads listing restaurants wherever you are at the touch of a button.'

'None of those devices have the "point of view" of a professional,' said Monsieur Pamplemousse soothingly. 'That is our great strength.'

'Try telling that to Madame Grante in Accounts,' countered Monsieur Leclercq. 'Times are hard for all of us, Aristide. Commercial travellers are no longer "on the road taking orders", but doing it from home placing their orders via the Internet. Even our nearest rival, Michelin, have had to vacate their prestigious premises in the avenue de Breteuil for a new address in Boulogne-Billancourt, beyond the Périphérique.'

The Director made it sound as though the

move was beyond the pale.

'A lot of well-known people live beyond the Périphérique,' said Monsieur Pample-mousse.

'Not after having been in the same building for well over a hundred years,' said Monsieur Leclercq. 'It is a worrying development, especially for an enterprise of their size and integrity. Their Director, Jean-Luc Naret, refused to go for a start. Now they have brought in an American who was born in Colorado. I fear the worst. Have you ever tried eating in Colorado, Pamplemousse?'

Monsieur Pamplemousse confessed the Director had a point. 'The founders, Édouard and André Michelin, must be turning in their graves,' he said. 'On the other hand, a growing number of people were beginning to think Michelin were failing to move with the times, and I have read that the newcomer is not only a lover of our country, but he spent some time working in a Michelin one-star restaurant and he even has a French wife. You could hardly ask for more.'

'All the more reason for us to look to our laurels,' boomed the Director. 'They have the name of their great tyre concern flying the flag for them. We rely entirely on sales of

Le Guide.

'Strictly between ourselves, Aristide, and I know I can trust you not to let it pass beyond these four walls for the time being, I have it in mind to move with the times and introduce what I believe is known as an app onto our website which will enable anyone with a mobile telephone finding themselves in a strange locality and wanting up-to-date information from *Le Guide* to do so on payment of a small fee.

'You may have encountered the newest member of our staff; a multi-talented, computer-literate individual called Barnaud. He is currently attached to Loudier, who as you know is approaching retirement.

'Barnaud has a degree in the electronics industry and his background is impeccable. It is he who put up the idea. I would like to move ahead as quickly as possible and to that end I am entrusting him with setting up a programme in time for next year's edition of *Le Guide*. He won't of course have details of all the changes that will be taking place with regard to the revised ratings of restaurants. Those, as always, will remain top secret until the day of publication, so that will be a last-minute affair.'

'Do you think that is wise?' ventured

Monsieur Pamplemousse. He couldn't help himself.

'Barnaud's own words,' said the Director. 'And that is what endeared him to me to and sealed the package.

'As proof of his integrity he phoned me later that same day and gave me the telephone number of the professor at his old university, insisting I shouldn't dream of going ahead until I had spoken with him.'

'And?'

'It was a direct line so I got through straight away, but proving my own identity turned out to be the hardest part. Once he accepted I was who I said I was he couldn't have been more helpful. He gave Barnaud a glowing report. I doubt if it could have been bettered. Then he, in turn, insisted on putting me through to the dean of the college, who confirmed every word the professor had uttered.

'In the meantime, until everything is up and running, *we* must learn to tighten our belts and learn to accept the world as it is, not as we would like it to be.

'Taking advice from Madame Grante I have ordered the fountain to be turned off during the night, and Rambaud, the gate-keeper, is starting work an hour later.'

Monsieur Pamplemousse supposed it must be a start in the right direction, however modest it might seem.

'Madame Grante does tend to look on the dark side of life,' he said. 'As for the Mafia; their tentacles spread far and wide, but in so far as France is concerned they were mostly rooted out in the early 1970s with the breakup of the so-called "French Connection" and the moving of the old heroin pipeline to the United States, which went via Marseilles, to Palermo in Sicily. The net result was that what up until then had been an impoverished island in the Mediterranean became one of the richest parts of Italy, although my understanding is they are currently suffering in much the same way as the rest of the world.

'But that doesn't mean to say we don't have our own crime gangs. Take the case of the major jewel robbery from Harry Winston's boutique in the avenue Montaigne. It took place in broad daylight and the total haul was valued at 85 million euros, no less.

'It was thought to be the work of an international gang at first, but everywhere these days there are wheels within wheels. Lips are sealed. Favours done. Two years later, 14 million euros of it was found hidden in a rainwater drain of a house in a Paris suburb.'

'Now Uncle Rocco thinks we owe *him* a favour,' the Director broke in gloomily. 'I strongly suspect he may have had that in the back of his mind when he made his arrangements. I wouldn't put it past him.

'I keep telling Chantal it wasn't confined to steaks. There are other scams going on as well in the restaurant world ... I have an example Uncle Rocco sent us to prove his point. It landed on our front desk two days ago: labelled URGENT and addressed to me. There was a brief note inside from him.'

Reaching down, he opened a drawer and withdrew a small package wrapped in silver paper. First of all he removed the outer covering and then he began unwinding several layers of greaseproof paper.

Pommes Frites leapt to his feet as an unmistakably earthy smell filled the room; a smell made all the more potent for having been confined to a relatively small space ever since its arrival.

His tail shot up, wagging furiously, while his lips began to salivate as he recognised the unmistakable scent of a truffle.

'Have you ever seen such a prime example of the *Tuber melanosporum*, Aristide?' asked Monsieur Leclercq, unwrapping the final layer of greaseproof paper to reveal a knobbly object the size of a giant lemon.

Monsieur Pamplemousse shook his head. 'Only in photographs, and some of those were probably blown-up out of all proportion, but this particular example of a "black diamond" has to be seen to be believed.'

'Think of the number of people who must have been seduced into ordering a truffle omelette when it was passed around the restaurant,' said the Director. 'It must have been worth its weight in gold to them.'

'Relatively speaking, of course,' said Monsieur Pamplemousse.

'When it comes to a truffle of these dimensions,' said Monsieur Leclercq, 'you cannot relate it to anything else on this earth, Aristide.'

'Or *in* the earth,' agreed Monsieur Pamplemousse. 'Always provided one knows where to look. They are God's gift to mankind.'

He had to admit it was the biggest, most beautiful specimen of a black Périgord truffle he had ever seen.

'It will seem almost a sacrilege when you come to eating it, *Monsieur.*'

'Alas, Pamplemousse,' said Monsieur Leclercq, 'I fear that is not to be. Uncle Rocco wants it back. I suspect he only sent it to me in the first place because he was seeking an expert opinion as to its validity. He is more familiar with the white Italian *Tuber magnatum* from Piedmont in northern Italy. The *tartufi bianchi* have a powerful scent. They can grow to the size of tennis balls overnight, but the downside is they need to be consumed straight away or they go into a steep decline. Besides, Italians tend to make use of them thinly sliced rather than cooked whole as we often do.

'Do you think this one is real, Aristide? Knowing the years you spent in the Food Fraud Squad of the Paris Sûreté, I had in mind seeking your advice on the subject. Time is of the essence. Meanwhile, having said that, I must guard it with my life.'

'A great deal of research has been devoted to the subject in recent years,' said Monsieur Pamplemousse, 'ever since Chinese truffles first appeared on the scene and for a while almost put paid to the European trade in the real thing. Then it was Moroccan Whites dyed black that went into a restaurant's omelettes, while the real thing, such as this proud example of the *Tuber melanosporum,* would remain untouched.

'There is now a national databank of the various molecules that combine to produce the aroma. It is possible to identify by means of DNA tests the area of the world they come from. For example, scientific studies show that the Périgord truffle in particular has a remarkably active sex life. Perhaps because it is French.'

'Must you bring sex into everything, Pamplemousse?' said the Director wearily.

'I think you will find, *Monsieur*, that one way and another, whether we like it or not, sex plays a part in most of the things we do in life,' said Monsieur Pamplemousse defensively. 'In many ways it is what makes the world go round.

'As always, the great Brillat-Savarin had very positive views on the subject. He maintains, and I quote: "Who says *truffle* pronounces a great word, charged with toothsome and amorous memories for the skirted sex, and for the bearded sex with memories both amorous and toothsome. It can on occasion make women more tender and men more apt to love."

'In the case of the Périgord truffle, you would be surprised at what goes on underground between the male and female elements. It has to do with what are known as pheromones: pungent sexual odours given off by the male when it wishes to attract a partner in the interest of increasing its spores.

Pigs do much the same thing when they want to attract a mate. It is all very basic. Whereas we humans spend any amount of money on perfumes which in the end make very little difference to our real selves, at certain times truffles exude a scent that speaks volumes to any passing dog or pig.'

'I would rather *not* think about it, Pamplemousse, thank you very much,' said Monsieur Leclercq. 'At least truffles confine their goings-on to below ground, unlike some others I could name.'

Monsieur Pamplemousse ignored the interruption. 'On the other hand, *Monsieur,*' he continued, 'one should beware of "truffle-flavoured" products, especially around Christmas time. *Par exemple,* cheap bottles of olive oil laced with so-called truffle aroma, when in fact what they really taste of is a synthetic chemical agent.'

'Ah, science,' said Monsieur Leclercq. 'It has a lot to answer for.'

'It brings us all down to earth at times,' said Monsieur Pamplemousse. 'On the other hand there is a great deal we must thank it for.'

'Tomatoes that look as though they have been grown in a laboratory, rather than a field,' countered the Director. 'All exactly

41

the same size, genetically modified groups of them snugly pre-packed into their standardised boxes; smelling and tasting of nothing because they have been developed solely for the benefit of the manufacturers, rather than the customers.

'What has become of those huge ones from Provence, Aristide? *Lycopersicum esculentum;* as shapeless as a Marfona potato; but oozing flavoursome juice?

'To take another example; all the year-round strawberries...'

Aware of a certain amount of movement at his side – the canine equivalent of drumming was the nearest way of describing it – Monsieur Pamplemousse hastily changed the subject while he had the opportunity. When Monsieur Leclercq was riding one of his hobby horses it was often hard to rein him in.

'Nature moves in strange ways its wonders to perform,' he said. 'We should not lose sight of the fact that during his time with the Paris Sûreté Pommes Frites was awarded the Pierre Armand Golden Bone Trophy for being best sniffer dog of his year. We still have it in a glass case at home. He is an expert in these matters, and we should take advantage of the fact.'

'What a splendid idea, Aristide,' said the

Director. 'I knew you wouldn't let me down.'

Pommes Frites pricked up his ears. He hadn't exactly been following the conversation. All he knew was it had been going on and on and on. So when Monsieur Leclercq picked up the plate on which the truffle reposed and held it out for him to see, it wouldn't have been overstating matters to say tears of joy and gratitude filled his eyes.

Even past masters in the art of illusion across the ages, from Heironymus Bosch to Siegfried & Roy, would have been hard put to explain quite how it happened, other than the well-known fact that the quickness of the hand can often deceive the eye, and there was no valid reason why a paw shouldn't be equally effective.

It was all over in a fraction of a second.

In short, there was no getting away from the fact that one moment it was on the plate, the next moment it wasn't.

CHAPTER TWO

Monsieur Leclercq hastily released his grip on the plate, and relieved of the weight of the truffle, which must have been considerable, it fell to the floor and broke in two.

'Did you see that, Pamplemousse?' he cried. 'Did you see it? Do something. Don't just stand there. *Do* something.'

In fairness, Monsieur Pamplemousse had been equally taken by surprise at the speed with which it had all happened. The truffle could hardly have had time to touch the side of Pommes Frites' mouth before it disappeared from view.

In common with bloodhounds the world over, he was possessed of a capacious mouth with jowls to match, so when the former was closed, the latter successfully concealed what lay beyond them.

Hopefully, he lifted the jowl nearest to him and peered inside.

'That's it, Aristide!' shouted the Director excitedly. *'Ouvre la porte!* Wait while I get a torch.'

'You can hardly call it a door,' said Monsieur Pamplemousse, stiffly. 'And there is no need for more light. All I can see is a row of white teeth.'

It was a wonder the truffle hadn't lodged in Pommes Frites' throat, but further inspection having revealed nothing of note, he released his hold of the jowl.

'What goes in must come out ... eventually,' he said lamely, as it fell back into place.

'*Eventually!*' boomed the Director. 'This is no time to be talking about *eventually*, Pamplemousse. It could be tomorrow, two days' time, or a week. I am talking about now. This very instant. Why can't we give him a good shake and see what happens?'

Monsieur Pamplemousse considered the pros and cons.

'As you wish, *Monsieur*,' he said dubiously. 'But I must warn you, Pommes Frites is no lightweight. The last time I put him on the scales he registered over fifty kilos. Besides, I don't have a plastic bag with me and I can't picture him taking kindly to being shaken without having one near at hand. He is a creature of habit and like most animals, when you try to make them do something they would rather not do, they become a 'dead' weight.

'Would *Monsieur* like to take hold of his head, or would you prefer to grasp what, for want of a better phrase, one might call, "the business end"?'

Monsieur Leclercq hesitated. Detecting signs of movement from the figure on the floor, he stood back.

'Perhaps you are right, Aristide,' he said grudgingly.

Having recognised several keywords in the Director's soliloquy and put two and two together, Pommes Frites was also having second thoughts.

Struggling to his feet, he headed across the room leaving a trail of minor rumbles somewhat akin to shock waves in his wake, rumbles that as ill luck would have it culminated in a major explosion at the far end of the room beneath a portrait of Monsieur Hippolyte Duval, founder of *Le Guide*.

It was probably a trick of the light, but as the sound echoed and re-echoed round the office it struck Monsieur Pamplemousse rather forcibly that Monsieur Duval's gimlet eyes, which normally appeared to follow you around the room, were concentrated on a waste bucket that stood to one side of the Director's drinks cupboard.

Breaking the silence that followed, Mon-

46

sieur Pamplemousse called Pommes Frites to his side. He put his arms round his waist and gave him a hug. 'There, there...' he said. 'Better out than in.'

Turning to the Director he endeavoured to make amends on behalf of his friend and mentor. 'In much the same way as when you warm a glass of cognac in your hands, the vapour given off is known as "The Angel's Share", *Monsieur*. So, when you hold a dog close to you, that, too, has a particular smell...'

'I shudder to think what that might be in Pommes Frites' case,' said Monsieur Leclercq. 'And if you are suggesting we open a bottle of Roullet Très Hors d'Age cognac to take the taste away, now is hardly the moment. You might at least train him to put a paw over his mouth when he does that kind of thing.'

'I doubt if it would have made the slightest difference in the circumstances,' said Monsieur Pamplemousse. 'Realistically, it would be a difficult manoeuvre at the best of times.'

'What do you mean...?' began the Director. Then, as the truth dawned on him, he made a dash for the windows and hastily flung one open.

'Must you always take Pommes Frites with

47

you wherever you go, Pamplemousse?' he demanded. 'We might have had company. Madame Grante going through the monthly expenses *par exemple*. I very much doubt if she suffers such problems with her Jo Jo.'

'The answer is "yes",' said Monsieur Pamplemousse stoutly. 'I do take him with me whenever I can. And with great respect, *Monsieur*, you were happy enough to seek his expert opinion on the validity of the truffle. Now you have the answer and it couldn't be plainer. As for Madam Grante's budgerigar, I very much doubt if it would consider itself in the running to compete with Pommes Frites. And even if it did, it wouldn't dare to. It would have fallen off its perch by now with its little legs in the air trying to avoid blotting its copybook in such an unseemly manner.'

He braced himself for the response, but realised he was clutching at straws. The Director was visibly deflated.

'*Touché*, Pamplemousse!' he admitted. 'Although, if you don't mind my saying so, there are times when Pommes Frites' methods leave a lot to be desired.'

He stood for a while staring out at the passing scene.

It was his habit at such moments to strike

a pose while making a passing reference to the Emperor Napoleon, whose body lay entombed in the Hôtel des Invalides further up the road, but for once suitable comparisons were clearly not forthcoming.

After what seemed like an eternity he turned away from the window.

'Forgive me, Aristide,' he said. 'I have a lot of things on my mind at the moment, and there is one other small matter which is causing me some concern.'

'Here it comes,' thought Monsieur Pamplemousse. True to form, Monsieur Leclercq had been saving the nitty-gritty, the main reason for his being called in, until last. In all likelihood it would be a case of for 'small matter' read 'ominously large'.

'To put it bluntly,' said Monsieur Leclercq, 'Chantal's Uncle Rocco is having trouble with one of his daughters.'

Monsieur Pamplemousse couldn't deny feeling a frisson of excitement at the news. 'Not Caterina?' he said. 'The one you asked me to escort from Rome to Paris a few years ago? If you recall we came up on the night train. The Palatino. They had done away with the restaurant car and replaced it with a buffet, so I was unable to submit a report regarding the standard of the cuisine.'

'The very same,' said Monsieur Leclercq. 'Escorted her all the way from Rome, Pamplemousse, and then, for want of a better word, mislaid her at the Gare de Lyon.

'She is travelling up from Milan and Chantal's Uncle Rocco would consider it a great favour if someone from *Le Guide* could be at the station to meet her. It seems he doesn't entirely trust her.'

'Not without reason,' thought Monsieur Pamplemousse. He wondered if he should tell the Director exactly what had happened on Caterina's previous ill-fated visit, but decided against it. It was a complicated story and there was a time and a place for everything.

Instead, taking a leaf out of Pommes Frites' book, he gave his friend a gentle pat and decided to await developments. In many respects it was much the easiest course. It didn't take much intuition on his part to guess the direction in which the conversation was heading. Patience was the order of the day.

Given that Monsieur Leclercq seemed to have temporarily lowered his guard, he returned to the attack.

'Regarding Caterina's unfortunate disappearance the last time she visited Paris,' he

50

said, 'it would be more fitting to say that for reasons of her own making, it was she who gave *us* the slip. Were he able to talk, Pommes Frites would vouch for the fact that it was a deliberate move on her part. It took us both by surprise. It was all the more surprising because until that moment Caterina and I had enjoyed our time together.

'As soon as the nuns who had delivered her to my keeping on Rome's Stazione Termini disappeared, she became a different person; almost as though a heavy weight had been removed from her being.'

Even more so, he reflected, by the time they went into dinner. Having replaced the regulation dark blue skirt reaching well below her knees with a fashionably short, dark red dress, she had looked breathtakingly beautiful.

'I still recall those "before" and "after" pictures you took,' said the Director, breaking into his thoughts. 'First the group photograph of her with the nuns on the station platform, then the one on the train before you dined. Quite extraordinary.'

Monsieur Pamplemousse felt tempted to add that even after all this time he still carried yet another photograph in his wallet taken *after* they had dined. With the top

51

button of her dress undone and a glow in her cheeks from the champagne, she had looked absolutely ravishing.

For a split second he wondered if he should show it to the Director, but he quickly decided against the idea. It was bound to be misinterpreted.

'Despite the fact that the Palatino's renowned travelling restaurant had been replaced by a run-of-the-mill buffet car, one way and another Caterina and I had a very pleasant journey,' he said. 'It was a disappointment, of course, but she was in high spirits. We even found ourselves laughing when I told her about the picture of a steak similar to the one we were eating, which was on display opposite the chef's galley.

'Presumably, as well as being there to titillate the taste buds of potential customers, it also acted as an *aide-mémoire* to the chef in case he had forgotten what it should look like when fully garnished.'

In fact, the only downside to the whole evening had been an Italian sitting on the other side of the aisle who had been listening in to every word of their conversation. Monsieur Pamplemousse had instinctively taken a dislike to him. It wasn't just the way he dressed: the pointed, impeccably polished black shoes, the loudness of his dark striped suit, or the matching brushed-back brilliantined black hair. It was simply because the man's eyes were hidden behind some impenetrable Bausch & Lomb dark glasses, making it impossible to outstare him. He had mentally christened him 'Il Blobbo'.

'It just so happens there was an unfortunate slip-up when we reached the Gare de Lyon and it was time to disembark,' he said. 'Pommes Frites and I found the corridor blocked by an American couple with all their luggage. It was like a small mountain, and by the time I managed to scale the lower slopes she had disappeared.'

'A flimsy excuse, Aristide. Especially for an ex-member of the Paris Sûreté,' said Monsieur Leclercq.

'In retrospect,' said Monsieur Pamplemousse, 'it didn't altogether surprise me. She was a spirited young lady, even though she was still at school. There was a strong streak of her father in her. I suspect she bribed the Americans to hinder our progress. They certainly did a good job.'

He paused, conscious of the fact that Monsieur Leclercq didn't know the half of it. Memories of his return to the Gare de Lyon later that day in a last-ditch effort to

53

find her came flooding back.

He had arrived at the Gare a quarter of an hour or so before the Palatino left for its return journey to Rome. Boarding had only just begun so he had been able to waylay the attendant who had served them on the way up from Rome. After a certain amount of questioning, the man revealed that on disembarking from the train, rather than make for the main exit, at his suggestion Caterina had used one of several smaller exits dotted along the length of the platform.

The man's words were still crystal clear in his mind. 'I think, Signor, she was trying to avoid someone.'

His embarrassment as he let fall the vital piece of information clearly showed who he thought that person was, which added a certain poignancy to the fact that less than half an hour later the Palantino was destined to leave Gare de Lyon for Rome without him, the driver being totally unaware that one of his colleagues was lying on a nearby railway line, the decorated head of a silver hatpin protruding from a bloodied right ear.

That there had been some kind of struggle was obvious; for alongside his body lay the trampled remains of some Bausch & Lomb dark glasses with one lens missing.

'*À quoi pensez-vous,* Pamplemousse?' said the Director. 'You appear to have something on your mind.'

Monsieur Pamplemousse weighed his options before responding. Which was it to be? A clear account of all that had taken place during Caterina's previous visit, or simply drawing a veil over the whole thing? He came down heavily in favour of the latter. Life was too short for such complications.

'Don't tell me something has happened to Caterina,' he said.

'Not yet,' replied the Director vaguely, as though he were choosing his words with care; placing undue emphasis on the word *yet*. 'Unfortunately, she has it in mind to spend some time in Paris.'

'*Oh, là, là!*' said Monsieur Pamplemousse.

'"*Oh, là, là!*" is right,' echoed Monsieur Leclercq.

'It is a nice time of the year to be here,' mused Monsieur Pamplemousse. 'Even Doucette's window box is showing signs of life.'

He couldn't help wondering why on earth he had been called in to be told something quite so mundane. There must be more to it than that.

55

'Late February and early March have their own charms,' he continued, playing for time. 'The leaves on the trees in the Tuileries are in bud...'

'Spring is in the air,' agreed Monsieur Leclercq. 'The fashion shows are in full swing ... not just in Paris, but everywhere in the world. Chantal has mentioned the fact to me more than once, and doubtless your wife has too...'

'Not that I have noticed,' thought Monsieur Pamplemousse. But if the girl was travelling up from Milan, the very epicentre of the world of fashion, that could be behind her visit. Perhaps his worst fears were groundless after all.

'We did discuss Caterina's future on the train,' he said. 'Her ambition was to become a fashion model after she left school – and with her looks and her figure it is easy to picture it all. She had everything worked out; first of all a spell of modelling; top models are in great demand and they earn big money. Then, assuming that was successful, she planned to open a boutique near the avenue Montaigne, or some equally suitable area in Paris. If that took off, there was the prospect of branches in other parts of the world; London, Berlin, New York... Japan ... even in

Milan itself.

'It struck me as being extremely pie in the sky, but she was so enthusiastic I had no wish to dampen her. We had a long discussion about the possibilities during our journey. I got the impression she wanted to unburden herself to someone other than her parents, who were not very sympathetic to the idea.'

'Not very sympathetic is putting it mildly,' said the Director. 'According to my wife, the very thought of Caterina parading on a cat-walk in scanty garments is total anathema to her Uncle Rocco.'

'The Mafia can be very uptight about their womenfolk displaying themselves to all and sundry,' said Monsieur Pamplemousse. 'They harbour old-fashioned views on such matters. It is probably why she was sent to a convent in the first place, although para-doxically, that had the opposite effect.'

'As I say, she had it all worked out,' he continued. 'And with her single-minded ap-proach to life and her father's backing, assuming he eventually relents, she could go far...'

'I have received a series of what you choose to call emails,' said Monsieur Le-clercq. 'While she is in Paris he suggests she stays, not in a hotel, but in our house.

'He feels she wouldn't be safe in a hotel, and it couldn't have happened at a more inconvenient time. My wife is on her way to Switzerland at this very moment visiting her mother, so apart from the staff I am all on my own. It wouldn't be right and proper to harbour a young maiden. I live in a small village and you know what small villages are like. Tongues would wag.'

Especially when that someone has set his sights on becoming the next mayor when the present one retires, thought Monsieur Pamplemousse.

He considered the matter for a moment or two. 'When you say she wouldn't be safe in a hotel, *Monsieur*, what do you mean...?'

'Exactly that, Pamplemousse,' said Monsieur Leclercq. 'According to her father she would be far from safe. There are those who would be only too pleased to see her fall under a bus...'

'In which case,' said Monsieur Pamplemousse, 'I would suggest a hotel bedroom is one of the safest places in the world to be...'

Monsieur Leclercq emitted a deep sigh. 'Please don't be difficult, Aristide,' he said. 'You know very well I was speaking metaphorically. In any case, his greatest fear is the possibility of the girl being kidnapped.

Kidnapped and held to ransom.'

'Are you telling me, *Monsieur*, that her father – a member of a noble Sicilian family, with connections here, there and everywhere – is unable to put his foot down and prevent her from travelling?'

'Have you ever tried telling a young girl she mustn't do something, Aristide?' asked the Director. 'It immediately has the opposite effect. Especially in this day and age. I have it on good authority it is what is currently known as "girl power", and there is a lot of that around these days; more's the pity.'

Not having fathered any children, Monsieur Pamplemousse had to confess be was unable to offer an opinion on the subject. Although Monsieur Leclercq must suffer the same disadvantage.

'Anyway,' he added lamely. 'The last time I saw her was several years ago, when she was still attending a convent school. She may well have changed by now.'

'I doubt it,' said Monsieur Leclercq. 'Convents are said to be among the worst breeding grounds for revolt. All those years sublimating girlish desires. Besides, age doesn't come into it. It starts earlier and earlier. Twenty-one years, sixteen, thirteen; they are all tarred with the same brush.

They are a danger to society, wearing skirts that are way above what is known in nautical circles as the plimsoll line; for all the world like those frilly window pelmets in houses of ill repute in days of old, or in present day Amsterdam come to that; an open invitation for those of like mind to enter.'

Monsieur Pamplemousse stared at the Director. It was unlike him to be so vehement on what was, after all, a run-of-the-mill topic.

'I have an English friend,' he said. 'You may recall my mentioning his name from time to time when our paths have crossed – a Monsieur Pickering. He is an expert in security and often quotes a phrase which I believe came originally from the Bible: "It is hard for thee to kick against the pricks."'

Monsieur Leclercq stared at his subordinate while he digested the thought.

'Not the happiest of synonyms, Pamplemousse,' he said at last. 'Why, only this morning I had a hair-raising experience on my way into the office when I encountered a bevy of young girls waiting to cross the road at some traffic lights.

'Egged on by the others, one of them turned her back towards me and actually had the temerity to lay her satchel on the pavement and bend over it as I drew near. It is little wonder my eyes began to wander. Unfortunately, I lost my concentration on the road ahead just as the traffic lights began to change.'

Removing a handkerchief from his top pocket, the Director dabbed at his forehead as he relived the experience.

'The net result was I shot the lights, which by then were at red, and in so doing nearly sent a *gendarme* flying. He was perched on a plinth in the middle of the junction directing the traffic. Luckily it didn't damage my car, and he managed to jump off it in time.'

'You are under arrest for dangerous driving?' hazarded Monsieur Pamplemousse.

'Fortunately no, Aristide. The man's gaze was fixed on the very same girl who, as I drove past her, was actually gyrating on the spot. At least he had the grace to pretend otherwise when he caught my eye. He simply waved a warning finger at me before beckoning her over. As I continued on my way I caught sight of him in my rear-view mirror. He already had his notebook out and was taking down her particulars. I trust he gave the girl a good reprimand.'

Monsieur Pamplemousse couldn't help

but wonder if he was after her name and address for reasons beyond the call of duty.

'I partly blame my choice of car, of course,' said the Director. 'It is the downside of driving a top-of-the-range Citroën. It attracts unwanted attention from the hoi polloi wherever I go.

'We live in an age when the have-nots of this world are only too anxious to despoil anything which comes within range of a knife point or a spray can. For that very reason I had to make use of the underground car park when I arrived this morning. It will cost the company a small fortune in *pourboires*.'

'By the same token,' said Monsieur Pamplemousse, 'it shows up yet another advantage of driving a *deux chevaux*. Apart from the fact that there is little about it that can be defaced, the possibility of making it easy to view ladies' *derrières* while on the move probably never occurred to its original designers.

'It certainly doesn't give rise to lascivious thoughts in the minds of passers-by, or other drivers for that matter. Unless they happen to be Americans, who find it hard to believe their eyes. People tend to look the other way when I drive past; girls especially.'

But Monsieur Leclercq clearly had other things on his mind. 'I do agree,' he said.

'Whoever coined the phrase "beauty is in the eye of the beholder" was speaking nothing but the simple truth.'

'I am led to believe it goes back to Ancient Greece,' said Monsieur Pamplemousse. 'The 3rd century BC. That is to say Before Citroën.'

'Well, there you are,' said the Director, ignoring the feeble attempt at a pun. 'The Greeks have an eye for these things.

'All of which doesn't solve our present problem. In spite of everything, Caterina is the apple of her father's eye. Chantal's mother is nearing 106 and hasn't long to go, so she daren't cancel her visit. My mother-in-law has become very forgetful in her old age and there is a problem as to whether or not she has made a will. It is exercising us considerably. In the meantime, apart from the staff I am virtually on my own.

'Tongues wag, Pamplemousse, and that is something I cannot afford to happen in my position. Beside which, I have *Le Guide's* reputation to consider and we are getting perilously near to publication, which is why my thoughts turned to your good self.'

Monsieur Pamplemousse did his best to look surprised at the sudden turn in the conversation. It was on his mind to say it would have been nice had the Director sought his views first, but he had left it a split second too late.

Monsieur Leclercq held up a hand to forestall him. 'Caterina's father thinks very highly of you, Aristide,' he said. 'Which is why I suggest you take over at this juncture.

'I know for a fact that in his view you tick all the boxes. You may be an ex-member of the Paris Sûreté, but the very reason for your having to take early retirement shows that unlike many of those who shared the same vocation, you have a human side to your nature. I refer, of course, to the affair at the Folies when you were caught scantily clad with a brace and bit in your hand.'

Monsieur Pamplemousse suppressed a sigh. There it was again. It would follow him around forever and there was no going back.

'How was I to know I had ended up immediately above the girls' dressing room prior to the first performance of the day?' he protested. 'The whole thing was a set-up. I doubt if any them would have cared two hoots if I *had* drilled a hole through the ceiling. There is safety in numbers and bare *derrières* would have been the least provocative objects on display.'

'That is no excuse to go *sans pantalons*,'

64

said the Director severely.

'I happened to loosen my belt,' said Monsieur Pamplemousse, 'and they fell down of their own accord.'

'There are those,' said Monsieur Leclercq, 'who might say with a certain amount of justification that it was a knee-jerk reaction programmed into your system and you had no choice in the matter.'

'It was a very hot day, *Monsieur*, and I was on the trail of what I had been told was an important clue in a case I was working on. Rather than bring disrepute to my colleagues in the force, I chose to take early retirement.'

'Unfortunately, mud sticks, Aristide,' said the Director. 'And it is often hard to remove. Nevertheless, I know it appeals to Uncle Rocco's sense of humour. He has often mentioned it to my wife over the years. Which is why I am sure he would be only too happy if you and your wife chaperone Caterina for the time being and afford her shelter as a guest.

'Another plus will be the fact that your apartment is in Montmartre, whereas I live beyond the Périphérique, and that would not suit Caterina at all. In her eyes it would be what they call "out in the sticks", which is not her scene. In common girl's parlance she would most likely say she "doesn't do sticks".

'Also, and correct me if I am wrong, Aristide, but as I recall, should it prove necessary, you have an escape route from your apartment block via an underground car park with a rear entrance and exit next door to you. You also have Pommes Frites to protect you in the event of any untoward happening.'

'I know what it is,' thought Monsieur Pamplemousse. 'Over and above any views his wife may have on the subject, the old shyster doesn't relish being on his own when Chantal's uncle discovers what has happened to his prize truffle, nor does he fancy having Caterina with him in case she is attacked and he has to take the blame for not looking after her.'

In fact, the whole affair was a bit of a mess-up. If Uncle Rocco hadn't got himself involved in the demise of the restaurant owner in the first place, he wouldn't be quite so worried about his daughter's safekeeping now.

'What am I going to tell Doucette...?' he began.

'My advice to you, Pamplemousse, is *nothing*,' said the Director. 'If my wife is anything to go by, the less you tell her the better. By and large, wives tend to go on about things, and once they get the bit be-

66

tween their teeth there is no stopping them. It is worse, far worse than a dripping tap.'

Monsieur Pamplemousse gave a wry smile. Communication might not be a strong point in the Leclercq household, but failing to tell Doucette the whole truth would be a far greater crime in her eyes than coming clean. He would certainly never hear the last of it if he followed the Director's advice.

'When exactly is Caterina expected to arrive in Paris?' he asked.

'This afternoon,' said Monsieur Leclercq. Opening one of the drawers in his desk he withdrew a pile of emails. 'We are supposed to be living in a paperless society, Aristide, but look at this one.' He held it aloft for Monsieur Pamplemousse to see. Apart from the words TRAIN FROM MILAN ARRIVES GARE DE LYON 13.23. CATERINA, the rest of the A4 sheet was bare.

Monsieur Pamplemousse looked at his watch. They had spent almost exactly an hour beating about the bush, and one way and another the even tenor of his life had taken a plunge. Quite how he had got there and how it would end up was something else again. It was a *fait accompli* and no mistake. Once again, he had fallen into a trap and it was too late to do anything about it.

67

'I will take up a position by the stairs leading up to Le Train Bleu restaurant,' he said. 'It is opposite the *quais* where trains leave and depart. If I station myself on the balcony at the top of the stairs it will give me a commanding view of the scene.'

'First-rate thinking, Aristide,' said Monsieur Leclercq approvingly. 'We don't want a repeat of the last *débâcle*, do we?'

'I know the place of old,' said Monsieur Pamplemousse confidently. 'And they say lightning doesn't strike the same place twice.'

Monsieur Leclercq rose to his feet. 'What would I do without you, Aristide?' he exclaimed, holding out his hand. 'If you make good time, you can kill two birds with one stone. By partaking of an early *déjeuner* you can carry out a spot check on the restaurant itself while you are waiting.'

'Trouble?' asked Véronique, as they made their way out via the outer office. 'I popped my head round the door earlier on but nobody even noticed. There seemed to be a bit of a commotion.'

'Trouble,' said Monsieur Pamplemousse.

'Anything I can do to help?'

'You could book a table for one at Le Train Bleu for some time after midday,' said Monsieur Pamplemousse.

'No Pommes Frites?' said Véronique.

'Sadly, no,' said Monsieur Pamplemousse. 'He is indisposed.'

Monsieur Leclercq's secretary glanced across at Pommes Frites as she reached for the telephone. 'Oh, dear,' she said. 'You poor old thing. That's not like you. Promise you will get well soon.'

'He nearly swallowed a *Tuber melanosporum* whole,' said Monsieur Pamplemousse. 'I think it is only temporary, but it was a very large one.'

'It sounds painful,' said Véronique. 'I'll light a candle for him on the way home tonight.'

She gave a sigh. 'In the meantime, guess who's going to be slaving over some hot proofs for next year's guide all day tomorrow? Blinds drawn, phones off the hook, strictly no visitors. It's decision time for the Stock Pot Brigade. I read out a list of the candidates while the Director listens and reaches his final conclusions. Last year there were twenty-six with three Stock Pots, over eighty with four, and not far short of five hundred with one.

'It doesn't end there. Think of all the additional information there is to sort out. Special Awards: Gold, Silver and Bronze Stock Pot lids for the best in their group.

Minor Awards in the way of symbols, like a tasting cup for an above-average wine list, or ear plugs for intrusive piped music. Not to mention those being downgraded.

'My mouth was so dry I got through two bottles of Châteldon.'

'It was Gertrude Stein who said that French people are unhappy when they are not entirely occupied with the business of living,' said Monsieur Pamplemousse. 'And at least Monsieur Leclercq has good taste in his choice of mineral water.'

'Enjoy your lunch!' said Véronique wistfully.

CHAPTER THREE

On his way home, with an unusually sombre Pommes Frites in the back seat of his *deux chevaux,* Monsieur Pamplemousse slipped a disc of Louis Armstrong's *What a Wonderful World* into the player to cheer himself up, after which he began rehearsing what he would say to his wife.

'Couscous, I have something to tell you,' was the easy bit. He had to admit that what came after it was more problematical. It depended on her reaction. He tried out a few possibilities...

'No, *chérie*, I have no idea how long Caterina will be staying...'

'She is really quite a simple girl, Doucette. Nothing to write home about.'

'No, Couscous, I doubt if she will get her *culottes* in a twist if you serve her croissants for breakfast. Her taste in food is very catholic...'

He made a mental note not to add the obvious rider should the question arise– 'Assuming she is wearing any' would be like playing with fire.

He could, of course, sweeten the situation by taking home a bouquet of flowers, but then again, suspicions might be aroused.

As for the Director ... he went over the conversation once again in his mind. All other matters aside, why didn't he come straight out with it and say his wife had put her foot down when he had told her the news? She must have done so with a vengeance. He could hear her voice; 'Henri! I'm not having you alone here with *that* girl...'

Switching over to the radio as the traffic slowed down at a junction, he turned up the volume to drown any possible noises coming from the back seat.

A man alongside him in an open car looked startled as the sound of Wagner's *'Ride of the Valkyries'* filled the air. Marrying Monsieur Pamplemousse's lip movements with the music, he raised his hat and accelerated on his way.

At which point they went over a bump, and as a precautionary measure Monsieur Pamplemousse reached up and opened the canvas roof of his car. Pommes Frites made as if to wag his tail, but immediately thought better of it. At least he had the decency to look the other way.

Slowing down as they joined the rue de Clichy near the end of the journey, Monsieur Pamplemousse completed the rest of it in a more leisurely fashion. Rather too leisurely as things turned out, for as the lift doors opened on the seventh floor of their apartment block in the Place Marcel Aymé he heard a vacuum cleaner going full blast.

It sounded as though Monsieur Leclercq had beaten him to it and already broken the news to Doucette. The old devil! After all he had said. Trust him to make certain there were no escape routes.

He was beginning to think that when it came to floors, seven was his unlucky number, and his worst fears were realised the moment he entered their apartment.

'Is it that dreadfully plain girl you escorted from Rome that time?' said Doucette. 'The one you managed to escape from as soon as the train reached Paris. She sounded as though she was no better than she should be.'

'That was a long time ago, Couscous,' said Monsieur Pamplemousse, guardedly. 'Remember, she was still at school. She had only just turned sixteen. Girls tend to branch out when they leave. That must have been a good four years ago. I doubt if I would even recognise her now she is no longer a teenager.'

'Didn't you tell me the last time she was in Paris her ambition was to set up a *pinarium* in the Place des Vosges along with some of the other sixth-form girls from her convent?'

'Not so much a brothel, *chérie*,' said Monsieur Pamplemousse. 'More of a *maison de tolérance*. Or a *maison clandestine*, if you prefer.'

Doucette unplugged the cleaner. 'Words! Words!' she said. 'What's in a name? They all amount to the same thing, and if she is anything like you say she is, she wouldn't have had many clients knocking at the door, that's for sure.'

'Not necessarily, Doucette,' said Monsieur

Pamplemousse. 'It wasn't her intention to be one of those offering her favours. As ever, she had it all worked out. It was to be in the best possible taste. A bar downstairs with champagne on the house for starters. Luxurious state-of-the-art rest rooms upstairs.

'For legal reasons, the *femmes de chambre* would be unpaid, but hopefully they would be lavishly tipped for their services. By any yardstick it has to be better than what I understand to be the latest haunt of the oldest profession in the world: day and night service from camper vans parked near the Périphérique in Saint-Ouen.'

'What about the Brigade Mondaine?' said Doucette. 'The so-called Paris Vice Squad. What were they doing at the time? Sitting on their backsides waiting to form a queue?'

'I got there before they did,' said Monsieur Pamplemousse simply. 'Besides, prostitution is still legal in France, provided you aren't caught moving while you tout for custom. The clampdown on smoking has dealt that kind of thing a blow. "Have you got a light?" provided a ready excuse to waylay any passing man and engage him in conversation. As for brothels, they no longer trade as such. Most of them simply have a little plaque by the door calling themselves Villa this or Villa that. Whatever springs to mind...'

'All that nous from a sixteen-year-old. It couldn't have come through reading *Vogue*,' said Doucette. 'She sounds a strange mixture and no mistake. I'm looking forward to meeting her even if she is no longer a teenager.'

Monsieur Pamplemousse was beginning to wish he hadn't told Doucette. Perhaps Monsieur Leclercq had a point after all.

'She's a simple girl at heart,' he said. 'I daresay when she hears what her father has planned she will get her *culottes* in a twist at the very thought of meeting you.'

'*If* she is wearing any,' said Doucette.

'Couscous!' exclaimed Monsieur Pamplemousse. 'How could you possibly say such a thing?'

'You can't take anything for granted these days,' said Doucette. 'You only have to think of that PIP scandal which was headline news while it lasted. Hordes of women going around Paris flaunting their *balcons* like nobody's business, and the implants turned out to contain waste factory material all the time.'

'I would rather not, Couscous,' said Monsieur Pamplemousse primly. 'There are enough disappointments in life as it is without adding to them.

75

'Why don't you come with me to the Gare de Lyon to meet the train?' he added, testing the water. 'We can have lunch in Le Train Bleu. The Director suggested I might give it a quick check before *Le Guide* goes to press.'

He knew he was pushing his luck, but it was infinitely better to take the bull by the horns while he had the chance and make a point about how much Caterina had changed since he last saw her.

Opening up *Le Guide's* issue case with the view of getting down to more serious business, he removed a Fujifilm X-Pro1 camera. He had been keen to get his hands on it. On the cutting edge of current design, it was the Director's latest essay into the realms of photography – presumably before his cost-saving plans had taken root.

Doucette shook her head. 'Pommes Frites will have to move out of the spare room and I haven't even started on that yet,' she said. 'The last time it was properly aired was after he had his friend to stay...'

'It wasn't *his* friend,' said Monsieur Pamplemousse. 'It was your doctor's schnauzer and they didn't get on at all well. As I recall it was badly in need of a bath and it kept us awake all night.'

Ignoring the interruption, Doucette paused

and gave a sniff. 'Talking of which, I can smell something strange, Aristide. Can you?'

'I'm afraid a truffle went down the wrong way,' said Monsieur Pamplemousse. 'At least, we think that's what happened. We've rather lost track of its whereabouts.'

'That's what comes of bolting your food, Aristide,' said Doucette.

Monsieur Pamplemousse caught Pommes Frites' eye, but mention of truffles sent Doucette off on another track. 'I must get some Italian food in...' she said. 'Where is the best place to go? You're the expert.'

Monsieur Pamplemousse had to confess he didn't know the answer off the top of his head. 'All I can tell you about Italian food is there are as many different shapes and sizes and kinds of pasta as there are days in the year. I could ask Loudier. Since he got near to retirement he's been dealing mainly with the Paris area. Or you could ask any Italian restaurant. Better still, why not go to La Grande Épicerie de Paris in Le Bon Marché'. They stock practically everything in the food line ... over 30,000 items at the last count as I recall.'

'At a price,' said Doucette.

'The Director can pay,' said Monsieur Pamplemousse. 'It's his problem after all.

But make sure you keep any receipts.'

He took a quick glance at his watch. 'If you can't come with me, I had better go. I'll leave Pommes Frites to mind the apartment for a change. He's had a bit of a setback and could do with a rest.'

From his position on the sidelines Pommes Frites registered his approval. Not so much because he needed a rest, but because he had 'things' on his mind; mostly to do with his experience in the Director's office. It was really a matter of a major breakdown in communication. It seemed to him that so far both Monsieur Leclercq and his master had been getting hold of what he had often heard them call 'the wrong end of the stick', and he needed time to consider what to do about it.

He wasn't sure if it had to do with the smell or the taste, or perhaps a bit of both, but it needed an explanation. And with that thought uppermost he made for the balcony.

Unaware of what was going on in Pommes Frites' mind, Monsieur Pamplemousse was somewhat relieved at having the problem of what to do with him while he was meeting Caterina's train taken out of his hands for the time being.

Automatically slipping his own Nikon

Coolpix S710 into a jacket pocket, rather than take *Le Guide's* somewhat bulkier camera, he set off down the hill to the nearest Métro station at Lamarck-Caulaincourt and the Line 12 train heading south.

At Madeleine he changed on to Line 14, with its state-of-the-art automatic driverless train. Although it had been up and running since 1998, he had never travelled on it before. Wedded to his car, as were nearly all his colleagues by the very nature of their work, he suddenly felt a schoolboyish excitement at the thought.

Ronald (call me Ron) Barnaud, *Le Guide's* newest recruit to its corps of inspectors, officially gaining unpaid work experience with Loudier, although others thought there was more to it than that, had lost no time in extolling its virtues over a glass of champagne when he had cornered Pamplemousse in the canteen bar. Quite why he had made the change from a supposedly flourishing career in the electronic industry no one knew. But then most of the inspectors had come from other walks of life. Truffert was ex-Merchant Navy. Barnaud had been in the wine trade. Guilot had written travel books, and still did on the side.

Given to wearing sunglasses even when he

was indoors, despite the time of year, had already earned Barnaud the nickname of Karl after the German couturier Karl Lagerfeld, who was rarely seen without them.

Guilot reckoned it was heliophobia.

'Indoors?' said Truffert. 'This time of the year?'

But there were other similarities to Monsieur Lagerfeld. The stiff, highly starched high collar shirts for a start, like city figures of old. And, as with Muslim ladies' veils, being unable to make eye-to-eye contact meant it was almost impossible to tell what Ron was thinking, although he more than made up for it by his enthusiasm and willingness to help others. He was into everything.

When Monsieur Pamplemousse, exercising his special relationship with the Director, tackled him on the subject on behalf of the other inspectors, he was suitably elusive.

'It was a chance encounter,' he admitted. 'Much as when you and I met, Aristide, except in your case our paths had crossed once before when you had rendered me a small service.

'With Barnaud it was the dark glasses he insists on wearing. He very nearly knocked me down as I was about to cross the road to my car, and since he was hovering on the edge of the pavement I thought I would do my good deed for the day. The sun was shining and I suppose I was in a sunny mood myself.

'It turned out he hadn't wanted to cross the road, but it broke the ice so I offered him a lift by way of recompense.

'When I asked him what he did for a living, he was somewhat circumspect. He let fall the fact that he was working for a government department engaged in top-secret electronic molecular research, whatever that might be. Apparently it is so hush-hush it hasn't even got a name, only a number and he wasn't at liberty even to give me that.

'He kept looking out of the back window, and at one point asked if I would mind doing a U-turn just in case we were being followed. I was so taken by surprise, I obliged, of course. I could hardly do anything else. And as my car went into a four-wheel drift I happened to say that by comparison my own work was very humdrum.

'He asked me what it was, and much to my surprise when I told him he suddenly became all ears. It transpired he was looking for a career move at the time and when I happened to mention our plans to widen the scope of *Le Guide* he grew quite excited and said it was just up his street.'

81

'And that was when you gave him the job?' asked Monsieur Pamplemousse.

'Not straight away,' said Monsieur Leclercq. 'During the course of our conversation I asked him all the usual questions. Why should I hire him? What were his biggest failings? Where did he picture himself in ten years' time? What would be his favourite meal were it the last one in his life?'

'And he satisfied you on every count?' said Monsieur Pamplemousse. 'How about his CV?'

'We shook hands on it,' said the Director simply. 'Again, much as you and I did. In my experience face-to-face encounters are often worth all the CVs in the world. Job applicants tend to glorify their past exploits on a CV. Office boys become office superintendents on paper. Very few people start off at the bottom of the ladder these days, and even if they do they are ashamed to admit it.'

At the time Monsieur Pamplemousse listened with only half an ear. He could hardly question the Director's judgement in the circumstances. He had been born and brought up in a world where such things as a CV were unknown.

'Another point in his favour,' said Monsieur

Leclercq. 'He happens to speak very good English, which could be of use if we ever branch out and produce a guide to English restaurants along the lines of Michelin. Slim volume though it might be.

'But in truth, even if Barnaud is only with us for as long as it takes to get the new programme under way it will have served its purpose.

'Between ourselves, as a cover I have let it be known that he is on a learning attachment with Loudier, but he has his own office and can come and go as he wishes.'

'And that has worked so far?'

'So far so good,' said the Director. 'There was only one little hiccup soon after he arrived. He said it was essential to have a list of all the changes to the new edition and when I said that was impossible he very nearly threw in the towel.'

But he didn't, thought Monsieur Pamplemousse as he changed trains, and here I am.

By Barnaud's reckoning the unique sound of the Météor's rubber-tyred arrival and departure in a station was music to the ears, and he could see at once what he meant. The smooth way it stopped in exactly the right spot so that the double layer of doors, those on the platform for the safety of the waiting passengers, and those on the train itself, could open and close in unison was, in his opinion, poetry in motion; a tribute to its designers, as was the ability to walk the entire length of the train down the central aisle while it was on the move at 40kph or more. At times – when it was on a particularly straight stretch – it could, if necessary, reach a speed of 80kph ... all controlled automatically by sensors on the track!

The fact of there being a complete absence of a driver's compartment at both ends of the train meant there was an unobstructed view ahead, whichever way it was going: a gift to any small boy (and for Ron too, by the sound of it), enabling them to play at being a driver to their heart's content.

And all of it watched over by staff comfortably seated in the control centre at Bercy, courtesy of a liberal sprinkling of closed-circuit cameras in each of the eight coaches that made up the train's full complement, thus ensuring the passengers' safekeeping.

But above all, again according to Barnaud, and not to be missed at any cost, was the sheer scale of the architecture in all the stations one encountered en route. Monsieur Pamplemousse had received his first taste of it at Madeleine as he approached banks of glass-sided escalators before descending into the unknown. Much as it went against the grain to be lectured on the capital's Underground system by someone from another part of France he couldn't help but look forward to the experience, and he wasn't disappointed. Châtelet, *par exemple*, had been like the setting for a James Bond movie.

It was a shame Pommes Frites was missing out on it all. But he was in no fit state to travel anywhere, let alone eat out. Welcoming glances from other passengers and diners alike would be thin on the ground.

Reflecting that everything in life has its downside, when they arrived at the Gare de Lyon Monsieur Pamplemousse was in too much of a hurry to do more than cast a fleeting glance at the giant tropical rainforest lining the side of the island platform; a scenic surprise which was only revealed in full when his train automatically went on its way towards the Bibliothéque François Mitterrand.

He had to give it to Barnaud. The fact that the whole system had been conceived and built in less than ten years was a miracle in itself, and equally miraculous though it was to see such lush vegetation flourishing so far underground he was too intent on following the signs pointing upwards to the *Grandes*

Lignes to give it more than a fleeting glance.

Then suddenly, as he stepped off the top of an escalator, he took a step back into the world as he remembered it. Ahead of him on the far side of the concourse stood the familiar curved stone staircase leading up to Le Train Bleu.

A *monument historique,* preserved for the nation thanks to the offices of American food writer M. F. K. Fisher and André Malraux, the French Minister of Culture at the time, France's leading *belle-époque* restaurant was as much a memorial to a bygone age as the train he had travelled on was unashamedly a symbol of the twenty-first century. Clearly Ron's technical wizards hadn't had things all their own way, and he couldn't help feeling relieved.

The station itself was far more crowded than he had expected. His old mother, had she been there, would have said 'I can't think where everyone's going', completely disregarding the fact that her being there at all made her one of the travelling public. Mixed in with it all there were security police with dogs, and a small detachment of men in military uniform – a sign of the times if ever there was one. There was also a sprinkling of SNCF staff wearing red-banded hats, presumably to shepherd any lost souls to wherever it was they wanted to be.

Although he didn't envy them their task, he couldn't help feeling another frisson of excitement as he looked up at the clock in the middle of the vast concourse. The hands were at 12.19, which gave him a little over an hour before the train from Milan was due to arrive.

Both sides of two giant display boards on either side of the clock appeared to show departures only, but as he climbed the steps leading up to the restaurant he caught sight of another board marked ARRIVALS high up on a far wall near where he had just entered the platform area. From where he was positioned most of it was obscured by a large hanging advert for cars, of all things. But it was sufficient for his needs. Running his eyes down what was visible in the first column he saw the 13.23 from Milan was already listed as being due to arrive on time. There was no need to look any further.

Having put his mind at rest, he entered the restaurant via a revolving door, and adjusted himself to the fact that it, too, was already more crowded than he remembered it ever being at that time of day, and he was doubly glad he had asked Véronique to book a table. At least it meant he would be seated in the far end of the main restaurant along with others who had made a reservation, while at the same time affording a good view of everything going on around him.

Making himself comfortable, he took cover behind a menu, the vastness of which was commensurate with the almost overpowering size of his surroundings. What was the size of the room? Something like thirty metres long by thirteen metres wide, and some ten or eleven metres high if he remembered aright. Anything smaller in the way of a menu would have been like the proverbial pea on a drum and totally out of place.

That, at least, hadn't changed and never would, so he spent the next few minutes studying what was on offer.

In the old days the barman was said to mix the best dry Martini in Paris, and *saucisson pistaché* was all the rage, but even if they were still available it was no time to put them to the test.

Scanning the options, he quickly ruled out both the 'Menu Dégustation' ... seven courses would be pushing it a bit ... as would the 'Menu Sarah Bernhardt'. Clearly, if the number of alternative dishes listed was anything to go by, the great actress of bygone times had never been in a particular hurry; probably she had been a regular customer when she was nearing retirement and was *en route* to her favourite watering hole in the country. Apart from the menu, she had even had a cake named after her – a doughnut, cream and chocolate mix, suitably primed with rum.

By process of elimination he settled for something far less complicated and ordered *soupe des asperges vertes glacée* along with a glass of champagne to begin with, followed by – possibly because his mindset was focused on Italy and the forthcoming meeting with Caterina – *cannelloni d'avocat et thon rouge,* and a glass of red Chianti.

While he was waiting for the arrival of the first course he sat back and took stock of his surroundings. It was good to relax for a minute or two and dwell on the richly decorated walls festooned with pictures of glamorous ladies and their escorts framed within carved and gilded curlicues.

Overflowing with nymphs, angels and satyrs, festooned with flowers and horns of plenty, female forms in all possible shapes and sizes and positions gazed down at him, or in some cases ignored him completely, being fully taken up with other more important matters closer to their heart.

Named after the legendary *Train Bleu*, which once upon a time ran every day between Paris and Ventimiglia on the Italian border, the mythological scenes were interspersed with landscapes painted in oils by a variety of artists of the 1900s, depicting the countryside it would pass through en route.

Above it all, partly hidden by giant chandeliers, lay Flameng's original painted ceiling.

Apart from the staff, nothing had changed in over hundred years, but somehow it always came out fresh.

A girl wearing a wedding dress suddenly put in an appearance and seated herself nearby. She was accompanied by an entourage of young men. There was no sign of a groom, so it was hard to tell if it was before or after the event, or perhaps she was simply taking part in a film, or a television series. It was all part of life's rich pattern, but from all around mobile phones with their inbuilt cameras recorded the scene as they came into play. Yet another sign of the times. Nothing was sacred any more.

He was on the point of reaching for his Nikon when the first course arrived. Had he been wearing his normal working clothes he would have automatically reached for his trusty notebook, secreted in a hidden pocket of the right trouser leg. One of Doucette's unique embellishments, he felt lost without it. As it was, he would have to rely on memory and a few scribbled notes on a blank page of his diary.

The asparagus soup was presented in a tall glass, the bottom half of which contained the main ingredient, while the top half was filled with a creamy concoction flavoured with Parmesan cheese. It was accompanied by a small pastry case of mixed herbs. He gave it six out of ten.

The house champagne came already poured and according to the menu was a Demoiselle Vranken Millesime 2003. It was a first as far as he was concerned, although glancing through the separate wine list he could have chosen many another had he wished.

So far, so good; better by far than many station hotels he had encountered over the years, and at least everything arrived with commendable speed.

That was one thing that *had* changed. Gone were the ancient slow-moving waiters of yesteryear. Service was brisk. The waiting staff, young, well drilled and clearly used to dealing with a clientele constantly on the move, could hardly be faulted. Carrying their fully laden trays with practised ease in one hand well above the heads of anxious departing passengers laden with luggage, there was never an impatient sideways glance.

His Cross ballpoint pen came into action again as he jotted 'poetry in motion' in his diary. Adding 10/10 for endurance and good grace, he fell to wondering how Caterina would have fared on her train. No doubt she had been travelling first class and by now she would be in the final stages of her long journey; brushing her hair, applying make-up, making sure she was ready to face the world.

Catching the waiter's eye, Monsieur Pamplemousse tapped his Jean d'Eve wristwatch as the man drew near. 'I am meeting someone off the 13.23 train from Milan,' he said.

The waiter raised one eyebrow and allowed himself a discreet sucking noise through his teeth. He glanced down as he cleared the table before hurrying off.

The meaning was clear. 'You are pushing your luck, *Monsieur.*'

'*Effronté*,' muttered Monsieur Pamplemousse. The cheek of it! Catching a train was one thing, but you didn't need running shoes in order to meet up with someone arriving after a long journey. They wouldn't be first off the platform. For two pins he would revise his award of 10/10.

All the same, he checked his wristwatch against the restaurant clock to make doubly sure they tallied.

The arrival of the main course, again in double-quick time, restored his good humour, and he ordered a mixed *glace vanille* and a *sorbet framboise* along with the bill to follow it.

'*Oh, là, là!*' said the waiter. 'Is that wise, *Monsieur?*'

'*Oui,*' said Monsieur Pamplemousse firmly.

'*Bonne chance!*' The waiter treated him with renewed respect. 'Perhaps the train will be late arriving,' he added brightly.

Monsieur Pamplemousse opened his diary and having jotted down: 'Waiter attentive, but of a nervous disposition', snapped it shut. Taking things as slowly as possible, he toyed with the glass of red wine. It helped dampen his growing irritation before starting on the cannelloni.

Normally he would have been the first to admit that his knowledge of Italian cuisine left a lot to be desired. It simply wasn't his field. That being the case, he eyed the large tube of pasta occupying the entire width of his plate with a certain amount of reserve. It could have been a bicycle-tyre inner tube for all he knew.

Somewhere in the deep recesses of his mind he remembered reading there were two ways of preparing the dish. Either the pasta was brought in and arrived that way or, and it was supposed to be the aficionado's approved method, the chef constructed a flat piece of pasta made up of a number of squares held together with béchamel sauce on which the filling was spread, before rolling it into a long sausage shape, much like a Swiss roll.

He tried lifting it up with a fork to see if there were any visible joins, and then, conscious that the waiter was watching his every move, briskly cut it in two. Time was precious, and his report to Monsieur Leclercq would have to take second place on the agenda. It was a matter of priorities.

The filling was predominantly a mixture of avocado pear, tuna fish, tomato and olives, held together by the béchamel sauce, and the pasta was yellow, suggesting eggs had been used in its making. There was a green salad on the side. All very acceptable.

The ice cream and sorbet came and went, as did the bill. Having paid by card, and with

a full three minutes to go, Monsieur Pamplemousse nonchalantly rose from the table and
sauntered out of the restaurant, stationing
himself fair and square in the middle of the
balcony at the top of the staircase.

Camera at the ready, he zoomed out, took
a couple of wide-angle shots of the scene
before him, and while pocketing it con-
verted the movement into a quick glance
over his shoulder.

His waiter was not so much engaged in a
deep conversation with a colleague, as in-
dulging himself in a display of shrugging,
hands at shoulder height, palms facing
upwards, that wouldn't have disgraced an
instructor in a school for the profoundly
deaf and dumb. As an encore the man made
the international sign for slitting someone's
throat before going on his way.

Returning to the matter in hand, Monsieur Pamplemousse pressed the playback
button on his camera and ran through the
pictures he had just taken. As he did so he
stiffened.

It wasn't possible! It simply wasn't possible!

Not only was every *quai* occupied by a sta-
tionary train, but there was a distinct absence
of any passengers either coming or going. He
ought to have registered the fact while he was

taking the pictures, but that was the down-side of having to rely on a small electronic screen rather than an optical viewfinder. Exterior lighting falling on its surface often rendered it worse than useless. He should have brought the Fuji X-Pro1 after all.

Racing down the stairs two at a time he waylaid the nearest SNCF representative.

'What happened to the train from Milan?' he demanded. 'Where is it?'

'Where is it?' repeated the man. He pointed towards the arrivals board on the far wall. 'If *Monsieur* would care to consult the *tableau des arrivées* he will see that it was scheduled to arrive in Hall 2 at 13.23. *Quai nombre* 7.

'Hall 2?' repeated Monsieur Pample-mousse. 'What do you mean ... Hall 2?'

'When was the last time *Monsieur* used the Gare de Lyon?'

'A few years ago,' admitted Monsieur Pamplemousse. 'I can't remember the exact date.'

'Ah!' said the voice of authority patiently. 'There have been major developments since then, *Monsieur*. The Gare de Lyon now has *trois* halls.'

'*Trois!*' echoed Monsieur Pamplemousse. 'What on earth for?'

Affecting not to hear him, the man

launched into what was clearly an oft-repeated explanation. 'We are at present standing in what is now known as Hall 1, which is for all French SNCF express TGV trains to and from the Côte d'Azur, the Savoy and the Alps.

'Hall 3, which is on a lower level, below Hall 2, is for all the Paris Underground services; Métro Lines 1 and 14, and RER Line A.

'Hall 2 is reserved for our foreign partners who run TGV International trains to countries outside France. That includes the one *Monsieur* was looking for: TGV France–Italie from Milan.

'It is a major improvement,' he added, catching the look on Monsieur Pamplemousse's face. 'Passengers no longer have to change trains at the border.'

Monsieur Pamplemousse reached for his wallet. 'Can you get me to Hall 2 as quickly as possible?' he demanded. 'It is very important.'

The man waved his gesture to one side. 'That is not necessary, *Monsieur*. It is part of my job. You are not the only one to be confused. It happens all the time.'

He glanced up at the arrivals board. 'The 13.23 from Milan is no longer listed, so it must have arrived on time. Alas!'

'Alas?' Conscious that he was in danger of turning the conversation into a repetition contest, Monsieur Pamplemousse stared at the man.

'Unfortunately, *Monsieur*, the *quai* is some distance from here. I can escort you, but it is not straightforward. The passengers will have dispersed by the time we get there.'

'I still wish to go,' insisted Monsieur Pamplemousse. 'The person I am meeting may well be waiting nearby.'

'Must be waiting,' he repeated inwardly, as the man led the way along the furthermost *quai*. '*Must* be waiting. It can't happen to me twice.'

His heart sank as they made a turn to the left and met up with a sea of people moving in all directions. Why on earth hadn't Barnaud warned him of all this palaver? He must have known about the change in the layout. Perhaps he was only interested in the electronics of the Mètèor Line anyway.

'Is it always this busy?' he asked.

'*Toujours*,' said the man, raising his hands heavenwards. 'Over 90 million passengers pass through the Gare de Lyon every year. *Autant chercher une aiguille dans une botte de foin.*'

98

'Pardon?' said Monsieur Pamplemousse, his mind preoccupied with higher mathematics.

'Finding someone is like... What is it *les Rosbifs* say? "Like looking for a needle in a haystack"? It is *impossible!*'

They went the rest of the way in silence.

'*Monsieur* is very quiet,' said his guide, as they came to a halt and he pointed towards *quai* 7, totally devoid of passengers.

'*Merde!*' exclaimed Monsieur Pamplemousse. It was addressed to the world in general, but it came out louder than he had intended. Heads turned.

'Is it very serious?' asked the man.

'I have been trying to divide 90 million by 365,' said Monsieur Pamplemousse.

'Someone else was asking me that only the other day,' said the man. 'The daily total is a little under 250 *mille*.'

'250 thousand!' Monsieur Pamplemousse wished now he had brought Pommes Frites with him. Given a brief sight of the picture he carried in his wallet he would at the very least have reduced the odds against finding Caterina down to a sizeable figure of rejections in no time at all.

Thanking the man for his trouble, he took a shot of the empty *quai* and followed that with a few random wide-angle shots of Hall 2 for luck and, if necessary, to back up his story, then found a relatively quiet spot and rang Doucette on his mobile.

Perhaps not surprisingly she was out, so he left a message on the answering service instead.

'There is a problem, Couscous. Don't wait up. Expect me when you see me!'

CHAPTER FOUR

After what could only be described as a personal *débâcle* to end all personal *débâcles* at the Gare de Lyon, the rest of the day was little short of a nightmare.

One by one, Monsieur Pamplemousse explored all the possible things that might have happened to Caterina, and the more he drew a blank the gloomier he became.

Being wise after the event, he realised, of course, that she should have been provided with his telephone number and/or address in case of a slip-up in the arrangements. But it had all come about so quickly it hadn't occurred to anyone to think that far ahead.

The last thing he wanted to do was phone Monsieur Leclercq in order to break the news. For all he knew, Caterina might have friends living in Paris she could contact, but that was something he couldn't bank on, and since standing still and doing nothing at all wasn't an option, he soon gave up looking around the station with its all too ample supply of restrooms and small cafés, and set about checking hotels in the area; a task that would normally have been passed on down to the newest recruit in any police force.

It brought back memories of his own early days as he methodically called on the most obvious ones first of all: the largest of those close by.

Stalwarts such as the Novotel Gare de Lyon, and the Mercure, took one look at Caterina's photograph and suggested his best plan would be to contact the nearest police station, as did most hotels of similar standing he visited in the area; a move that wouldn't have gone down too well with either Monsieur Leclercq or his wife's Uncle Rocco, both of whom discouraged what they would have called unnecessary publicity.

Having whittled down the obvious possibilities, he turned his attention to what might be called the 'also rans'; the second-

and even third-rate possibilities. Not that he expected Caterina to lower her sights, but simply because it was what combing an area was all about. It was 'all or nothing at all'. You couldn't afford to make exceptions.

If it did nothing else, it brought home to him a sad fact of life commonplace the world over. For one reason or another, large railway termini tended to attract unsavoury characters, and historically the Gare de Lyon was certainly no exception to the other Paris terminals.

Both the Gare du Nord and the Gare de l'Est had been credited with lowering the social status of their area of the 10th *arrondissement* even before they were built; and the Gare Montparnasse, having attracted an influx of hopeful girls from Brittany in search of fame and fortune, soon turned the streets of the 14th into a notorious haunt of prostitutes.

But long before the advent of the railway, the part of the 12th *arrondissement* where the Gare de Lyon now stood had been deemed a 'no-go' area. Known latterly as Paris's Chinatown, it became a drug-infested slum area of narrow alleyways, frequented by criminals of the very worst kind, its one claim to fame being the fact that it was once home to the infamous Mazas prison.

So it wasn't too surprising that showing Caterina's photograph around should meet with a totally different reaction to the one he had experienced until then, ranging from total indifference, through suspicious owners who clearly thought they might be laying themselves open to a trap of some kind, down to hearty denials of there being any possibility that the hotel might let rooms by the hour. The last mentioned was usually followed by a nudge, a wink, the dangling of a key, and the information that of course there were always exceptions to any rule.

In desperation after the tenth such encounter – or was it the eleventh? He was beginning to lose count – he decided to ring Jacques, an ex-colleague in the Sûreté, and an old friend.

At first, Jacques was less than helpful. On hearing Monsieur Pamplemousse's tale of woe, he cheerily launched into a story about Ernest Hemingway's first wife Hadley. Having packed the only copies of everything he had ever written, both published and unpublished, into a suitcase, she set off to join him in Lausanne where he was on an assignment for the *Toronto Star*. Leaving the case momentarily unattended in a train at the

Gare de Lyon, she returned only to find it had been stolen.

'Can you think of anything worse?' asked Jacques.

'Orson Welles not only lost his screenplays, but all his films and other creations when his villa in Madrid burnt down in 1970,' said Monsieur Pamplemousse.

'Just think,' said Jacques, not to be outdone. 'Hemingway only had an old Corona portable in those days, and yet he set to work straight away retyping everything from memory at the rate of five hundred words a day. *And* he had to work standing up, because he suffered from a bad back.'

'I imagine the air was blue,' said Monsieur Pamplemousse.

'It didn't do the marriage a lot of good either,' admitted Jacques. 'But at least he ended up winning the Nobel Prize for his writing, which is more than any of those who tried imitating his methods at the time can say. Most of them didn't stay the course. Mind you, he was a perfectionist. When he got to the end of *A Farewell to Arms* he dithered for ages over some forty or so possible titles.'

Sensing a lack of enthusiasm in his audience for the problem in hand, Monsieur Pamplemousse changed tack.

'Which reminds me,' he said. 'I was going to phone you about a Mafia-type murder of a restaurant owner that took place recently in the 3rd. His body was found floating in the canal St Martin.'

'It doesn't ring any bells,' said Jacques. 'But he wouldn't be the first one to end up that way by a long chalk. Do you have a date?'

Monsieur Pamplemousse picked on one that as near as possible tallied with the Director's tale of woe.

'Leave it with me and I'll see what I can find out,' said Jacques. 'In the meantime I suggest you watch where you're going. The area you're in at the moment isn't much better after dark. It may have come up in the world, what with all the *grand projets* they've gone to town on: Mitterrand's Bastille Opera, the Palais Omnisports, and Frank Gehry's American Center, to name but a few. But you can't lose sight of the fact that their roots are embedded in tainted soil that will take years to regain its good health.

'All I can say is watch your back when you get in the car.'

'I don't have the car with me,' said Monsieur Pamplemousse. 'I came by Métro.'

'Then get Pommes Frites to act as a look-out,' said Jacques. 'You need eyes in the back of your head these days, Aristide.'

'For once, I don't have him either,' admitted Monsieur Pamplemousse. 'I'm on my own. I must phone you again when I need cheering up,' he added, breaking the silence that followed.

'Feel free,' said Jacques cheerily. 'Always happy to oblige. But don't say I didn't warn you. I won't place a firm order for the flowers yet.'

Undeterred, Monsieur Pamplemousse carried on for a while longer until the Métro had stopped running. Quite frankly, he was off his normal beaten track and had lost his bearings. Had Pommes Frites been with him he would have automatically left his own personalised mark at regular intervals so that he would have had no difficulty whatsoever in retracing their steps. The great Designer in the skies had seen to it that canine's bladders were uniquely formed in order to cope with such situations. But he wasn't available and there was no point in wishing otherwise.

By the time he got back to the 18th *arrondissement* his apartment block in the Place Marcel Aymé was plunged into darkness, and none of it felt more so than the corridor on the seventh floor. Lourbet, the *gardien*, must have been in one of his public-spirited 'save on electricity' modes, so it was doubly pleasurable to find Pommes Frites waiting for him just inside the front door.

It would have been hard to say who was the most pleased by the encounter. Tails wagged, licks were distributed, fur ruffled, whispered greetings exchanged.

A small table lamp had been left switched on, presumably for Pommes Frites' benefit, and underneath it there was a note, decidedly not intended for his friend and companion. It said, quite simply: 'Please try not to make too much noise'.

Worn out from his perambulations, more than a mite dispirited by receiving such an uncharacteristically crisp message from his wife, overcome by an overall sense of failure, Monsieur Pamplemousse slumped down in the nearest armchair, closed his eyes, and with Pommes Frites at his feet, they were both soon fast asleep.

The next thing he knew was a familiar hand on his shoulder shaking him awake.

'Wake up,' said Doucette. 'I have so many things to tell you. First of all, Monsieur Leclercq needs you in his office urgently, only this time it really is an *Estragon* situation.

107

He's phoned twice, so it must be serious.'

'What!' Rubbing his eyes, Monsieur Pamplemousse leapt out of the chair, immediately thinking the worst. 'I must go at once...'

'Oh, no, you don't, Aristide!' said Doucette firmly. 'You can't go anywhere until you've had a wash and brush-up and a change of clothes. You look as though you've been pulled through a hedge backwards. Besides, it didn't sound to me as though it was life-threatening and I have lots of other things to tell you over breakfast.'

Monsieur Pamplemousse knew better than to argue, and it was a little over half an hour before he reappeared, freshly groomed, and ready to face the world again. Even Pommes Frites looked impressed by the change in his master's appearance as he eagerly led the way into the kitchen. Clearly, he had some important news to impart.

Although forewarned, Monsieur Pamplemousse couldn't have been more surprised by the change that had taken place during his absence. There were packets, boxes, tins and bottles everywhere ... it was like the inside of a grocery store.

'You were absolutely right about the Bon Marché, Aristide,' said Doucette. 'They couldn't have been more helpful...'

'But...' Monsieur Pamplemousse was at a loss for words.

'Would you like to hear the list?' said Doucette. She unfurled a long sheet of flimsy paper. 'Take cheese ... there's *Parmesan, mozzarella, ricotta* and *Gruyère*. Then there is *Arborio* rice for risottos ... they have so many different kinds ... tinned tuna, nutmeg ... according to the assistant who was serving me they use nutmeg in practically everything, and he was Italian, so he should know. *Prosciutto* ... *porcini* mushrooms (dried) ... *fagioli* beans ... *lasagna al forno. Pancetta* and *Parma* ham ... *panettone...*' She pointed at the table. 'That's an all-purpose cake. It keeps forever.

'My friend said that more than any other cuisine, Italian is only as good as the quality of the ingredients, and theirs is as good as they come. He says Bologna is the richest gastronomic region ... I think that's where he comes from. But he suggested I have a good selection of various kinds of pasta, along with the sauces to go with them.'

Among some bottles of wine on one of the shelves Monsieur Pamplemousse caught sight of a familiar Black Rooster insignia on one indicating a Chianti Classico; alongside it there was another familiar bottle.

'And Marsala?' he asked. 'We don't normally have any need for that.'

'I'm told it is indispensible in a good many Italian dishes,' said Doucette. 'Stews and ragouts ... marinating veal ... that kind of thing.

'He was very enthusiastic. It was hard to resist. Do you think I have bought too much, Aristide? It did include free delivery.'

'I only hope you've got a receipt for it all,' said Monsieur Pamplemousse.

'This is it,' said Doucette, unfurling more paper.

'The Director will have a fit when he sees it,' said Monsieur Pamplemousse.

'He knows already,' said Doucette. 'I used my credit card to pay, but I needed a guarantor, so I telephoned him. He couldn't have been nicer. *And* he's cleared it with Madame Grante in Accounts.

'I made my first real Italian dish yesterday evening,' she continued proudly. 'Tomato soup with pasta shapes.' She pointed to a bowl on the table. 'All it needed was a tin of chopped tomato, some chopped onion, carrot and celery. Sugar to taste, along with hot vegetable stock, and a handful of basil leaves from our pot on the balcony. There's some left over. You can have it now if you like.'

Monsieur Pamplemousse hesitated. Tomato soup with pasta shapes in it was the last thing he fancied for breakfast.

'No *brioche?*' he said.

'Pommes Frites had the last one,' said Doucette. 'There's plenty of *panettone*. Try that. There is an old Russian proverb. "A mouthful of seawater gives you a taste for the ocean."'

'Ah,' said Monsieur Pamplemousse, non-committally.

Cutting a slice of the Italian bread, he placed it in the toaster. It was so light he hastily drew back in case it caught fire.

As he did so he caught sight of the contents of the bowl and having spotted a neat row of pasta *x's* half submerged across the surface, he immediately felt bad at having declined the offer. It was no wonder Doucette had gone to bed early. Left on her own with what was probably meant to be a surprise homecoming for him gone to waste, what else was there for her to do?

'I daren't hang around, Couscous,' he added, by way of apology. 'Save it for tonight. My only hope is that it doesn't all come to nothing,' he added, buttering his toast. 'If it does we shall be eating pasta for a month of Sundays.'

Doucette stared at him. 'I really don't see why it should, Aristide.'

111

Monsieur Pamplemousse glanced at his watch. He had no wish to go into the reasons as to why it might very well turn out that way. He would cross that bridge when the time came.

'*Estragon* calls!' he said. 'I really must go.'

And having kissed his wife goodbye he was on his way with Pommes Frites, now fully recovered after his sleep, hard on his heels, before Doucette had a chance to say any more.

'Thank goodness you've made it,' said Véronique, as he entered her office. '*And* Pommes Frites! Is he feeling better now? I haven't got anything for him, I'm afraid.'

'He's recovered from whatever it was,' said Monsieur Pamplemousse. 'He has already had a *brioche*, thank you very much. We stopped on the way in.'

'*Parisienne* or *Nanterre?*'

'*Nanterre*,' said Monsieur Pamplemousse. 'It's his favourite.'

'Mine too,' said Véronique. 'I admire his taste.'

'In Pommes Frites' case I suspect it's because it happens to be the bigger of the two,' said Monsieur Pamplemousse. 'The thing is, he's had something on his mind, and when that happens his ears begin to sag and he can look very lugubrious.'

'Oh, dear,' said Véronique. 'Well, he's come to the right place. We're all pretty lugubrious this morning.'

'Tell me the worst,' said Monsieur Pamplemousse.

'Hortense swears the object in the waste bucket next door is a hand grenade and she refuses to have anything to do with it.'

'I don't believe it,' said Monsieur Pamplemousse. 'With all due respect to Monsieur Leclercq's cleaning lady, when did she last see a hand grenade?'

'Apparently her father was in the Resistance during the war,' said Véronique. 'He still keeps a row of them on his mantlepiece in case things ever take a turn for the worse. If they do, he'll be ready and waiting.'

'And that merits being classed as an *Estragon* situation?'

Véronique lowered her voice. 'You know the Director. You haven't heard the half of it yet. When Hortense first went into his room to empty the bucket, she put her head inside it and swore she could hear ticking, but I think it must be that dreadful wristwatch she insists on wearing.'

'The freebie she was given when she took

113

out a year's subscription for an American magazine she never reads because it isn't in French?'

'The very same,' said Véronique. 'She passes it on to me now and I don't read it either, but for a different reason. It's all to do with big business.'

'Hand grenades don't tick,' said Monsieur Pamplemousse.

'I told her that,' said Véronique, 'and what do you think she said?'

Monsieur Pamplemousse shook his head.

'Famous last words!'

'They do seem to be a remarkably gloomy family,' said Monsieur Pamplemousse. 'I think Pommes Frites and I had better go next door and see it for ourselves.'

'I wish you would,' said Véronique. 'She keeps telling me it has to do with what *les Anglaise* call Health and Safety, and I keep telling her we have the same thing over here only we don't always abide by it like they do. Life is too short. We've reached an impasse. They do say that in England at Christmas time even Papa Noël has to wear a seat belt when he is doing the rounds on his sleigh.

'Apart from that, the Director keeps ringing through wanting to know if the Bomb Disposal Squad have arrived yet. I daren't tell him I haven't even phoned them...'

'Leave it to me,' said Monsieur Pample-mousse.

'*Bonne chance*,' said Véronique. 'Hortense's last bulletin was "Mark my words, if the smell is anything to go by that grenade must have fallen in some *merde*."'

Monsieur Pamplemousse was about to signal all systems go to his assistant, but Pommes Frites beat him to it. Clearly, he was only too eager to get down to work.

'Aristide!' exclaimed Monsieur Leclercq, as Monsieur Pamplemousse entered his office. 'I thought you were never coming.'

Looking slightly embarrassed, he removed an old tin hat he was wearing. 'A precautionary measure,' he explained. 'I must admit it has been an unhappy experience. I haven't been able to get to my drinks cupboard all the morning for fear of setting off some kind of fiendish clockwork mechanism.'

Monsieur Pamplemousse took in the rest of the scene at a glance. The far end of the Director's office was cordoned off by a length of yellow crime-scene tape, and the waste bucket, still upright, was in much the same position as he remembered it.

'Careful!' called Monsieur Leclercq, as Pommes Frites made a beeline to it. 'We don't want him blown sky high.'

'I think he knows exactly what he is doing,' said Monsieur Pamplemousse. 'He's been wanting to tell me something ever since we got back home yesterday. I don't doubt the patron saint of bloodhounds, St Hubert, will be looking after his interests.'

Following on behind, he removed the offending tape before joining Pommes Frites who had his nose buried in the bucket, his tail fully erect and wagging slightly.

'I think he's trying to tell me something,' he said. 'I know the signs.'

'Perhaps we could try that BowLingual device you gave me that time,' said the Director. 'I still have it in my drawer.'

'I think not,' said Monsieur Pamplemousse. 'As you know, it's made in America and dogs speak a different language over there. If you recall, when you shouted "Wuff! Wuff!" at Pommes Frites in the Pommes d'Or Hotel that time, he misunderstood what you were saying and in his confusion he wouldn't stop barking. He had to be smuggled out in a laundry basket.'

Joining Pommes Frites, he peered into the bucket. 'I see what Hortense meant. It does smell of *merde*. It must be the underfloor heating.'

'*Merde?*' cried the Director in alarm. Reaching for the tin hat, he pushed his chair away from the desk. 'Whatever next, Pamplemousse? Think what might happen to my carpet if it explodes.'

Oblivious to Monsieur Leclercq's cries of alarm, Pommes Frites removed the offending object from the bucket and presented it to his master, who in turn crossed the room and placed it on Monsieur Leclercq's blotting pad.

The Director eyed it dubiously. 'Are you sure it hasn't been near some kind of noxious substance, Pamplemousse?'

'I know exactly what it is,' said Monsieur Pamplemousse. 'Or rather what it *was*. An excellent example of *faux* food.'

'*Faux* food!' repeated the Director. 'You mean such a thing actually exists...'

Monsieur Pamplemousse stared at him. For someone who was head of France's premier food guide, Monsieur Leclercq could be very unworldly at times, but then he probably only ever dined in Three Stock Pot restaurants.

'It is a long-established industry in Japan,' he said. 'I believe that in Tokyo there is a whole street devoted to the products. Normally they are used as window dressing in shops and occasionally restaurants, but most of all as props in stage productions and films, when they have to withstand a lot of wear and tear. They used to be made of wax before World War II, but nowadays they are mostly hand-made from vinyl chloride. No wonder we were all taken in, although clearly Pommes Frites had second thoughts.'

'Don't tell me he swallowed this in its entirety,' said Monsieur Leclercq, taking a closer look at the object.

'Hardly,' said Monsieur Pamplemousse.

'Then what was responsible for all the unfortunate noises he was making on his way to the waste bucket?' said the Director.

Monsieur Pamplemousse gave a shrug. 'Various minor bits may have become detached when he dug his teeth into it, causing some kind of chemical reaction. We shall probably never know. The Japanese guard their secrets well.'

'But the odour,' said Monsieur Leclercq. 'I would have sworn on oath that it came from a real truffle.'

'Ah,' said Monsieur Pamplemousse. 'Now we are entering another area which has made enormous progress since the war. The world of chemical compounds and the production of aromas. The elite exponents of the art are known as "flavourists", much as those in the cosmetic industry are called "the nose". The main difference is that flavour affects the taste as well as the smell. A whole industry has grown up on the back of fast food. The human nose is a powerful interpreter of aromas, and without a suitably attractive scent most of the products manufactured in today's food chain would die a death.'

'On the basis that to lose both the taste and the smell at the same time is little short of a disaster,' boomed the Director.

'*Exactement*,' said Monsieur Pample-mousse. 'They are the two main essentials which attract people to them in the first place and they need to be introduced by fair means or foul. The downside is that basically many of the products are responsible for the current growth in obesity.'

'How do you know all these things, Pam-plemousse?' said Monsieur Lerclercq.

'It is an important part of my job, *Monsieur*.' He felt tempted to add 'those of us on the road need something to occupy our minds between filling in forms', but it would have been a waste of breath.

'Ah, yes, of course,' said the Director vaguely.

'I have to admit that was the main thing

119

that bothered me about Uncle Caputo's truffle,' continued Monsieur Pamplemousse. 'The scent was almost too good to be true. Truffles tend to lose their characteristic odour fairly rapidly if they are kept for any length of time without being preserved in some way.

'On the face of it,' he mused, 'a giant truffle could be a profitable investment for a restaurant. As you so wisely said when we first set on eyes on it, one sniff on its round of the customers in a basket is all that would be needed to start the orders flowing.

'Perhaps,' suggested Monsieur Pamplemousse, 'Uncle Caputo realised that fact and having acquired a fake one, wanted to test it out on experts to see if they were taken in?'

'In that case we must order another as quickly as possible,' said Monsieur Leclercq. 'Although having said that, it is not a practice we ought to encourage.'

'I doubt if it will be possible anyway,' said Monsieur Pamplemousse. 'Would *Monsieur* happen to have a penknife in his desk drawer? Mine is in the issue case for safe-keeping,' he added, pre-empting the question as to why he didn't have it on him. In truth it was so heavy it destroyed any suit pocket practically on sight.

'Of course,' said Monsieur Leclercq. Opening a drawer, he produced a Victorinox Champ Swiss Army knife and handed it over.

Selecting a tiny wood chisel out of the thirty-one assorted blades at his disposal, Monsieur Pamplemousse set about probing the remains of the object on the Director's blotter, and after a moment or two what appeared to be a small red vein was revealed.

'You see what I mean, *Monsieur*. It is clearly the work of a master craftsman and these things take time. It is as much like a truffle as it is possible to get, and probably costs as much or more than the real thing.'

'This is disastrous,' said the Director. 'Most likely Caterina is charged with its safe return. We cannot possibly wait around any longer than is necessary.'

Sensing a possible opportunity for creating some breathing space, Monsieur Pamplemousse decided it was time he took the plunge before Caterina resurfaced. With luck he might be able to turn his unhappy experience to everyone's advantage.

'Has *Monsieur* been to the Gare de Lyon recently?' he enquired.

'I am happy to say, Pamplemousse, I have *never* been in the Gare de Lyon,' replied the

Director, not without a touch of pride.

'There are hectares and hectares of it to negotiate,' said Monsieur Pamplemousse. 'It is almost beyond measure. If you culled all the passengers running to catch a train because they were lost and haven't allowed sufficient time, you would gather enough people to fill a sizeable stadium in no time at all. It isn't so much a case of losing someone. It is a matter of finding them in the first place. How people ever manage to meet anyone by arrangement is beyond me.

'I was talking to a member of staff only yesterday, and he quoted an English aphorism to me: "It is worse than looking for a needle in a haystack."'

'A typical Albion obfuscation,' said Monsieur Leclercq dismissively. 'They are past masters in the art of creating smokescreens in order to divert attention.

'I must admit I could hardly believe my ears when I first heard the news of yet another failure in your mission, Pamplemousse, but since we are on the subject of Albion attitudes to life it prompts me to paraphrase the words of one of their most famous writers: Oscar Wilde. "To lose one young lady in a railway station may be regarded as a misfortune; to lose the same lady a second time looks like gross carelessness."

'As for comparing it to looking for a needle in a haystack, it would be singularly inappropriate to have a haystack in the Gare de Lyon, and once again typical of *les Anglais*.

'We are talking of a nation whose inhabitants are supposed to measure the contents of their wine glasses in terms of units. Can you imagine a Frenchman asking a lady friend if she would care for another unit?

'What was the man doing with a needle in a haystack in the first place? If I were a farmer catching sight of someone exploring my haystack and on being questioned he said he was looking for a needle, I would telephone the local *gendarmerie* immediately and have him arrested on the spot.'

Monsieur Pamplemousse was beginning to wish he hadn't brought the subject up after all, but he persevered.

'With respect, *Monsieur*,' he said, 'the phrase is of ancient lineage. Before the nineteenth century it used to be a simple bale of hay rather than a complete stack. It only goes to show the world has become ever more crowded, and the Gare de Lyon is a prime example of that fact.'

Monsieur Leclercq fell silent.

'I suggest we forget the whole thing,

Aristide,' he said after a suitable gap. 'All is well that ends well, and the fact that Caterina is safely ensconced with your wife means we can all rest in peace.'

Monsieur Pamplemousse stared at the Director, hardly believing his ears. He was shattered; momentarily struck dumb.

'She had my telephone number,' explained Monsieur Leclercq. 'Luckily I happened to be in when she called, so given that I was in no position to offer her a bed, I gave her your home address.

'Cheer up Aristide,' he said, when he saw the look on Monsieur Pamplemousse's face. 'Wives! They have their funny little ways, like butting in when you are the middle of telling a story with some totally inconsequential comment such as: "It wasn't a Wednesday morning, darling, it was a Thursday afternoon," and in so doing they lose sight of the whole. By the same token they keep things to themselves, and when you remind them of the fact they say: "I told you that days ago!"'

'But...' began Monsieur Pamplemousse. His mind went back to breakfast that morning. Doucette could have told him then. Perhaps she was saving the best until last and, rushing out as he had, he didn't give her the chance? He was suddenly filled with remorse as he recalled the row of kisses across the soup. Perhaps they had been from Caterina, not Doucette? From all he could remember, he wouldn't put it past her.

C'est la vie...

Declining the offer of a Roullet Très Hors d'Age cognac to celebrate the availability at long last of a safe passageway to the drinks cupboard, he bid Monsieur Leclercq *au revoir* and with the latter's undying thanks echoing in his ears, beat a hasty retreat into the outer office.

'Success?' Véronique looked up hopefully from her desk.

'Comme ci, comme ça,' said Monsieur Pamplemousse. 'It is all relative.'

'Relative enough for me not to phone the Bomb Disposal Squad?'

'They wouldn't thank you if you did.'

'It never occurred to me that they might,' said Véronique. 'So where to now?'

'Home,' said Monsieur Pamplemousse. 'There has been a major breakdown in communications.'

'Oh, dear, what's new?' sighed Véronique. 'There is either too little communication in this world or there is much too much. And sometimes too little can be caused by there being too many options. Have you heard

Bernard's latest tale of woe?'

Monsieur Pamplemousse confessed he hadn't. Bernard lived in Mortagne-au-Perche, and when he wasn't 'on the road' he was usually at home tending his roses. Their paths hadn't crossed of late.

'As far as Bernard knew,' said Véronique, 'his parents enjoyed a blissfully happy married life; some sixty years or more together with never a cross word.

'When his mother died, his father used to come and stay with his son and daughter-in-law from time to time, and it became very noticeable that he was extremely keen on biscuits. So much so, that when Bernard's wife was doing her shopping at the local *supermarché* prior to one of her father-in-law's visits, a girl on the cash desk, catching sight of all the packets in her shopping basket, said: "Your father-in law must be coming to stay."

Bernard thought this was rather funny, and he repeated the story to his father.

'"Ah," was the answer. "But you see, your mother never knew I liked biscuits, so I'm making up for lost time!"

'Can you imagine?' said Véronique. 'All those years together and he never once told his wife he was partial to a biscuit or two, and in all those years she never asked him if there was anything special he would like.'

'I think my problem is a bit more complicated than that,' said Monsieur Pamplemousse. 'But on that happy note...'

'Perhaps I should call the Bomb Disposal Squad after all!' said Véronique. 'Would you like me to give them your address?'

'Don't you dare,' said Monsieur Pamplemousse. 'I have enough problems as it is.'

CHAPTER FIVE

On the way home Monsieur Pamplemousse turned Véronique's sorry tale over in his mind.

Bernard's parents may have been blissfully happy, and there was a good deal of truth in the old saying 'ignorance is bliss', but it was a classic example of a total lack of communication; or perhaps more accurately, a lack of total communication. And who was the most to blame? The father or the mother?

Had they still been alive, Bernard would have been only too pleased to communicate his father's love of biscuits to his mother, but then his father probably hadn't mentioned the fact to anyone else, including Bernard, or they would have willingly done it for him.

Come to that, if he liked biscuits so much, why didn't he ever go out and buy some for himself?

One thought triggered another. Was it possible he and Doucette were in danger of going the same way? Could their own communication, or lack of it at times, be at fault, like that of Bernard's parents?

Monsieur Pamplemousse sincerely hoped not. Partly it had to do with his work, of course. Being away a great deal, often for weeks at a time, meant that when he was back home, apart from taking Pommes Frites for his morning walk, he often wanted nothing more energetic than to put his feet up. But then, Doucette must often feel that way too.

Other occupations threw up much the same problem. In his experience chefs were among the very worst off. Working for hours on end over a hot stove, day in day out, arriving home after midnight tired out, could undermine even the happiest of relationships. Musicians, too, were often away for long periods at a time when they were on tour...

But other people's problems were academic and beside the point. He must deal with his own first of all.

That was easily enough said. When was the last time he had offered to help in the kitchen? Or make the bed? Or do the ironing? To say that Doucette was so much better at all these things than he was and he didn't like to interfere was stretching things a bit. The fact was, as in most households, such matters had fallen into place early on in their marriage, almost as part of the natural order of things.

'Start as you mean to go on,' his old mother would have said. 'To each his own.'

To that end he tried out a few well-chosen platitudes on his audience of one, but for once he might just as well have saved his breath. Pommes Frites had his mind set on other things. He pricked up his ears every time he heard the word 'biscuits' mentioned, but when nothing edible was forthcoming he settled down again. However, he couldn't help noticing the key word was usually accompanied by a shrug.

Once or twice his master took both his hands off the steering wheel in order to make some meaningless gestures while he shouted *Sacrebleu!* at the top of his voice; a phrase he usually kept for other drivers who for one reason or another had upset him.

'*Une connard*' was another of his favourite expressions when someone tried to cut him up, especially when they succeeded, but that was conspicuous by its absence, so things couldn't be all bad.

In any case, for the time being they were of little moment. His own thoughts were still centred on the matter of the truffle, and clearly his master's words were meant for someone else. To his way of thinking it was all a matter of communication, or lack of it.

Monsieur Leclercq must have thought it was a real truffle, otherwise he wouldn't have offered it to him on a plate, and certainly he had seemed most upset when he, Pommes Frites, had taken him at his word. Perhaps he should have regurgitated it onto his desk there and then, instead of into the waste bucket?

There was no telling with humans. Sometimes they said one thing when they meant quite the opposite. Often they didn't even tell you what they wanted. He wouldn't have changed places with another dog for all the bones in the world, but there were times when even his master occasionally fell short in that respect.

A good example was the occasion when, without so much as a by-your-leave, he had attached a small object to Pommes Frites' head. Admittedly he had gone to the trouble of making a special harness so that it wouldn't fall off, but it was undignified to say the least. Worse still, he had been sent out wearing it while they were staying at a hotel in the Auvergne on one of their trips. Luckily it was after dark.

The fact that it was a tiny television camera didn't mean anything to him at the time, nor would it have done even if he had been told, so how could he have possibly known his cavortings with another hound he met up with quite by chance would be seen by anyone else who happened to be in the area? In colour as well! Besides, to a dog, even if they did move, pictures without any kind of smell attached to them meant nothing at all.

The way everybody kept going on about it afterwards, you would think such a thing had never happened before. When his master was talking about it, he had said something about Pommes Frites meeting up with a 'dog of the opposite persuasion', whatever that might mean. But his new acquaintance certainly hadn't needed any persuading. She had entered into the whole thing with a gusto the like of which he hadn't encountered for a long time. The whole episode had been mutually agreeable.

Even the other dog's owner had seemed more than pleased, shouting and blowing a whistle as though urging them on to make the most of the encounter. It wasn't often you met up with such an understanding owner, so both parties did as they were bidden, and were all the better for it.

Pommes Frites closed his eyes as he relived the moment, and he didn't come out of his reverie until he found himself standing alongside his master in the lift when they arrived home.

'Couscous,' said Monsieur Pamplemousse, as they entered the apartment together. 'Can you ever forgive me?'

'I might,' said Doucette. 'It all depends on what you have done to merit forgiveness.'

'Neglect,' said Monsieur Pamplemousse. 'Neglect of the very first order. Putting work before everything else, as ever.'

Doucette gave a sigh. 'I told myself a long time ago that's what comes of marrying a policeman. There has never been a truer saying than "Once a *flic*, always a *flic*", and this morning's call-out was a good example. What was all the fuss about? You've been gone for hours.'

Monsieur Pamplemousse dived in as quickly as possible with a rundown on all that had transpired since he and Pommes Frites had left the apartment that morning.

'Hardly an *Estragon* situation,' said Doucette, when he had finished. 'All that fuss over a truffle, and a fake one at that!'

'You know the Director,' said Monsieur Pamplemousse. 'He may have been born into a stratum of society that is automatically endowed with many advantages, but in some respects it might just as well have taken place on the moon. It bears little relation to your world or mine.

'As for his cleaning lady, she is living proof of the fact that truth is stranger than fiction. I doubt if Hortense has ever seen a truffle, let alone one large enough to be mistaken for a hand grenade. It is no wonder she thought the worst had befallen her.

'Do you know what the Director's last words to me were before I left him?'

'"What kept you, Pamplemousse?"' suggested Doucette.

Monsieur Pamplemousse shook his head. 'No. "You are an extraordinary *homme*, Aristide. The way you remember other people's

133

names. I wish I had that faculty. I shall forget my own name one of these days." He probably sees Hortense every working day of his life, too!'

'There are times when I wonder how you stand it...' began Doucette.

'I know, I know,' said Monsieur Pamplemousse. 'But nobody is perfect, and I must admit I had other things on my mind. *Par exemple:* at this moment in time there is nothing I would like better than a biscuit.'

Doucette gave him a strange look. 'You only have to ask, Aristide,' she said. 'I'll get you some as soon as I go out. What sort do you fancy?'

'Your choice,' said Monsieur Pamplemousse. 'Just as long as you get me some. You will never know how happy it will make me.'

'You *are* in a funny mood,' said Doucette.

'It must be catching,' said Monsieur Pamplemousse. 'I was expecting the Director to blow his top over my having messed up on meeting Caterina at the Gare de Lyon. It was hardly my fault, but even so I was prepared for the worst and he took it remarkably well.'

'You should have had a piece of cardboard with her name written on it in large letters,' said Doucette. 'You could have held it up in the air like taxi drivers do when they are meeting someone off a train. I wish I had thought of it before you left. It wouldn't have taken five minutes.'

'A fat lot of good that would have done,' said Monsieur Pamplemousse. 'I might just as well have been back home with you. I would have needed a rocket-propelled taxi to get me to the correct platform in time.'

'Think how poor Caterina must have felt when she arrived and there was nobody there to meet her,' said Doucette. 'Not that she complained to me. I tried phoning you back, but there was no answer.'

Monsieur Pamplemousse ignored the interruption. 'You could have knocked me down with a feather when Monsieur Leclercq told me she had been here all night.'

'And prior to that, for most of the evening while we were waiting for you to come home,' said Doucette. 'She was tired out after her long journey, so in the end we gave up. As soon as we had had our dinner she went to bed. As you may have gathered I put her in Pommes Frites' room. You got my message, I hope?'

'The one under the lamp telling me not to make too much noise?'

'And the one in the soup,' said Doucette. 'I used up all the *x*'s there were in the packet

of alphabet pasta. Don't tell me you didn't
see them.'

'It is one of the reasons why I didn't eat it
up there and then for breakfast,' said Monsieur Pamplemousse virtuously. 'I wanted to
leave it just as it was before it went soggy.'

It only went to show how careful one
should be about these things, and that one
should not put two and two together too
hastily and end up making five.

'She turned out to be such a nice girl,' said
Doucette. 'Not at all as you described her.
Really very attractive, I thought.'

'It's a long time since I last saw her,' said
Monsieur Pamplemousse hastily.

'Even so, I can't picture her getting up to
all the things you told me about.'

'Still waters run deep, Couscous.'

'There was nothing still about that girl,'
said Doucette. 'It almost felt as though she
was on edge about something. She couldn't
wait to help me in the kitchen, and she was
so interesting about her time at school.

'I have always pictured nuns living on bread
and water, but when she talked about quite
simple dishes such as the ones they prepared
in the convent ... things like pumpkins,
enriched with chopped pistachio nuts and
scented with cinnamon, she made it sound

like an ambrosial feast.'

'It depends to some extent on how hungry you are, Couscous,' said Monsieur Pamplemousse. 'They do say "He who would enjoy the feast should fast on the eve."'

'I quote, but apart from the slice of toasted *panettone* this morning I haven't eaten anything since this time yesterday at the Gare de Lyon. Which reminds me, I must fill in my report.'

'Well, you needn't think you will be getting any pumpkins for today's lunch,' said Doucette. 'It's macaroni cheese.'

Monsieur Pamplemousse's good intentions of being a model husband plunged momentarily. Given all the ingredients that were on display he was secretly hoping for something more adventurous. A *cannelloni* filled with cheese and lemon, perhaps. Or a *linguine* with saffron sauce.

'Giovanni said I should start with something simple,' explained Doucette. 'He called it learning to walk before I run.'

'Giovanni?' repeated Monsieur Pamplemousse. 'Do I know him?'

'He was the lovely man who served me in the shop,' said Doucette.

'Ah!' said Monsieur Pamplemousse. 'There is another Italian saying he might know,' he added hopefully. '"Hunger makes beans taste like almonds."'

'In that case I'll do some *borlotti* beans to go with the macaroni cheese,' said Doucette. 'Giovanni loves Tuscany and apparently Tuscans are addicted to them. He said beans often come in useful, so I bought several tins. If you buy them dried they have to be left to soak overnight and even then they need to be boiled for three hours. It's a good thing he told me.'

'I think perhaps I will have it as it comes,' said Monsieur Pamplemousse dryly.

'He was a mine of information on pasta,' said Doucette. 'Did you know that good-quality pasta made from wholegrain flour not only contains iron and potassium, but magnesium, copper and zinc too?

'Iron and potassium are good for the blood. Copper is good for the heart, and zinc helps the immune system fight infection.'

'Let us hope ours never goes rusty,' said Monsieur Pamplemousse. 'That's all I can say.'

'Don't tell me you're jealous, Aristide,' said Doucette. 'You had better watch out, it also contains a small quantity of manganese and Giovanni says that produces sex hormones.'

'He sounds like a walking nutritionist

pushing his luck,' said Monsieur Pamplemousse. 'If he eats all those things he must
be as fit as a fiddle.'

'Actually,' said Doucette, 'he's shorter than
me and rather fat with it. He had a job
reaching the top shelf. I had to help him
down. He did linger over the last bit.

'As for the macaroni cheese ... it's almost
ready. How would it be if I *soufflé* it?'

'Ah,' said Monsieur Pamplemousse. 'Now
you are talking, Couscous. You can set that
to music. Let *me* lay the table for a change.'

'While you're about it you can set that to
music too,' said Doucette.

Removing the macaroni cheese from the
oven, she reached for a copper bowl, added
some whites of egg, and set about whisking
them until they began to form a peak. 'The
cutlery is in the second drawer down,' she
called. 'In case you didn't know.'

'I'm looking for the corkscrew,' said Monsieur Pamplemousse, rummaging in the first
drawer while his wife busied herself adding
her mixture to the macaroni cheese before
folding it over and returning it to the oven.
'I thought it would be nice if we opened that
bottle of Chianti Classico on the shelf. It's
from Tuscany, so we can't go far wrong. In
the words of the old song ... the two will go

together like a horse and carriage.'

While Doucette busied herself with the plate warmer, he poured the first of the wine. It was from the house of Radda and at first taste the opulent flavour lived up to its reputation of being like a velvet fist in an iron glove. It boded well.

'In the meantime,' he said, 'what news of Caterina?'

'She had to go out. Important business. She didn't say what or where.'

'So she won't be joining us for lunch?'

'It didn't sound like it,' said Doucette. 'She said she had an appointment.'

Monsieur Pamplemousse didn't know whether to feel pleased or sorry. Part of him had been looking forward to seeing her, but just at that moment in time he was perfectly happy leaving things as they were.

'It's good you got on so well yesterday evening,' he said, as Doucette brought the dish to the table.

'She couldn't have been nicer,' said Doucette. 'Nothing like I expected ... not that I thought I wouldn't like her,' she added hastily. 'I must say she was very smartly turned out: a simple black dress, but immaculately cut. Italian design at its best. Matching shoes, a Bottega Veneta sling-bag, necklace, wristwatch ... all topped off with a bright red hat. You couldn't have missed her in a crowd.'

'Don't rub it in,' said Monsieur Pamplemousse.

'I wasn't meaning to. It is simply that it was the kind of outfit you normally only ever see in magazines. At least, in our part of the world.'

'And dream about? Or is it your turn to feel jealous?'

'Not really,' said Doucette. 'You need the lifestyle to go with it. Besides, Paris chic involves breaking the set rules and I wouldn't have felt at home. Aside from the red hat it lacked the offbeat finishing touch. I didn't feel in the slightest bit dowdy.'

'I should hope not,' said Monsieur Pamplemousse. Thinking about it, Caterina had been wearing a red hat when they first met at Rome station. He wondered if it could possibly be the same one.

'She could have brought me down to earth quite easily if she had wanted to.' Doucette broke into his thoughts. 'But I don't think it would have occurred to her. *And* she made her own bed this morning.'

'Convent training,' said Monsieur Pamplemousse. He topped up their glasses. 'It leaves its mark in more ways than one.'

'All that, and she was as happy as a pig in clover helping with the cooking. I think it took her mind off whatever it was that was bothering her.'

'I would be willing to bet she couldn't make anything half as nice as this,' said Monsieur Pamplemousse, diving into his lunch. 'Wait until it's Pommes Frites' turn to sample it.'

'The sobering thing is,' said Doucette, 'you would lose out. There seems to be no end to her culinary talents. You didn't warn me she cooks like a dream.'

'I didn't know,' admitted Monsieur Pamplemousse. 'We have only ever dined together once and she didn't cook the meal. It was on the train coming up from Rome.'

'Well,' said Doucette, rising from the table. 'Just wait until you've tasted the next course. From now on, Aristide, courtesy of Caterina, it will be my *pièce de résistance*.'

She crossed to the stove. 'For this I need a double boiler, four egg yolks – it's lucky I had some left over from the soufflé, and...' She consulted a sheet of paper. 'The zest of half a lemon, vanilla essence, granulated sugar, 180g of caster sugar, a little Marsala wine from that bottle you were so sniffy about, and a few minutes to myself.'

'Nothing would please me more, *chérie*,'

142

said Monsieur Pamplemousse.

And while Pommes Frites set about polishing off the remains of the first course, he sat back and watched Doucette busying herself at the stove for the following quarter of an hour.

'*Buon appetito!*' he exclaimed, when she eventually arrived back at the table carrying two dessert bowls, one in each hand.

It was followed a few moments later by '*Brava! Bene!* There is only one word for it, Couscous: *Parfait! C'est parfait!*'

Doucette flushed with pride. 'I must confess Caterina went through it with me last night,' she said. 'In fact, I have another confession to make. I hope you don't mind, Aristide, but you left *Le Guide's* camera out before you went off to the Gare de Lyon yesterday, and I used it to take a picture of her at work on it. It was the only time I saw her looking cross. I hope I didn't offend her.'

'If the picture is half as good as this *zabaglione*, I promise to have it framed,' said Monsieur Pamplemousse. 'It deserves a Three Stock Pot rating in *Le Guide*. It's a real dessert of the old school,' he enthused. 'A return to normality. Your Giovanni is right about one thing: Italian cuisine remains basically simple across the board and depends almost entirely on the quality of the ingredients. You could say out of all the cuisines in the world it is the most unchanging.

'By comparison, French cuisine is very labour intensive; I spend a great deal of my life ordering desserts, without having the faintest idea what they will look like when they finally arrive at the table. Generally speaking, even the most basic of dishes such as a *crème brûlée* will have been transformed into something Gauguin or Renoir might have aspired to. It comes from being out on a limb, apart from the hustle and bustle of the main kitchen. Pastry chefs these days live in a creative world of their own; a thing apart from the rest of the meal. They feel the need for recognition and it is one of the reasons why our cuisine remains the most creative in the world.'

'You don't have to eat what they give you, Aristide,' said Doucette.

'But I do,' he said. 'It is all part of my job, Couscous, and there is no escaping the fact. Aside from that, as you know, there is not only a part of me that wants to end a meal with a sweet taste, but I also think how awful it would be for a pastry chef if everyone in a restaurant reached the end of their main course and declared they were so full they couldn't eat any more.'

Monsieur Pamplemousse finished his dessert with a flourish while it was still warm. It was too good to waste and it wouldn't keep. Then, having offered to help with the washing up – an offer that won him bonus points, but rather to his relief was refused point blank – he retired to his 'den'; a small room tucked away in a corner of the apartment where he kept various items of computer equipment which enabled him to maintain contact with *Le Guide* and at the same time keep up with his hobby of photography.

It had been his intention to file the report of *Le Train Bleu* while it was still fresh in his mind, but what with one thing and another he soon became immersed in technicalities. 'I still can't get over what happened,' said Doucette, when he finally emerged carrying *Le Guide's* Fuji camera. 'I do hope Caterina is all right.'

By way of reply, Monsieur Pamplemousse opened up a compartment in the base of the camera and withdrew a small card.

'I have made a postcard-size print of your visitor,' he said, 'and it's most impressive. But I thought you might like to see something larger than life.'

Crossing to the television receiver in a

corner of the room, he switched it on, slid the card into a tiny slot below the bottom of the screen, and reached for the remote controller. Moments later a head-and-shoulders image of the girl filled the screen.

'It's what is known as an SD card,' he explained.

'I didn't even know such things existed,' said Doucette. 'It's uncanny … creepy almost. It feels as though she is still in the room, larger than life and twice as beautiful.'

'The composition is excellent,' said Monsieur Pamplemousse. 'Poetry in motion, you might say. And given it was taken in artificial light, the colour is surprisingly good. A few minutes' work with an editing programme and it wouldn't disgrace the front cover of *Le Guide's* staff magazine. Only one thing bothers me…'

'Don't say it isn't properly focused,' said Doucette. 'I thought it was on automatic.'

'So it was,' said Monsieur Pamplemousse. 'The focus is spot on … it is extraordinarily sharp … the highlights in the eyes are perfect … so much so, they only underline the fact that we have a major problem on our hands. There is no escaping one simple, but very worrying fact…'

'Don't keep me in suspense,' said Doucette. 'I promise never to use your camera again.'

'Unwittingly,' said Monsieur Pample-mousse, 'you may well have done us all a favour, Couscous. Quite simply, the girl in the photograph isn't Caterina.'

CHAPTER SIX

Doucette took a lot of convincing the girl wasn't who she said she was. In the end Monsieur Pamplemousse was forced to produce proof positive.

'It just so happens that as a precaution and to jog my memory in case she really had changed a lot, I took an old photograph with me.'

Reaching into an inner pocket of his jacket he reluctantly removed his wallet and made a show of looking through it several times as though he couldn't immediately find what he was looking for. Eventually he located a dog-eared postcard-size picture and having mentally braced himself for the worst, held it up for inspection.

'Poor girl,' he said. 'It was such an embarrassment for her. She had lost the top button of her dress and she hardly knew which way to look.'

Doucette made a grab for it.

'Two things, Aristide,' she said, holding it up to the light just out of his reach. 'Number one. I agree with you it most certainly bears little resemblance to the girl on the screen. The one who was here yesterday. Number two. It bears even less resemblance to your description of Monsieur Leclercq's niece. You are always telling me the camera cannot lie, so which version do I believe?'

'You are absolutely right in all you say, Couscous,' said Monsieur Pamplemousse. 'Traditionally the camera cannot lie. But there are times when, given the right circumstances, the *moment critique* as Cartier-Bresson used to say, it can transform the mundane into a positive work of art, as happened with the photograph you took of our visitor at the stove yesterday. That was a Cartier-Bresson moment if ever I saw one.'

'You didn't even meet her,' said Doucette. 'So how can you be so sure?'

'I have no need to meet her,' said Monsieur Pamplemousse. 'It is a gut feeling. We all of us see the world through different eyes, as I learnt to my cost many times

148

during the years when I was with the Sûreté. Take a dozen different people who have witnessed a crime and ask them for a detailed description of the villain. You will get a dozen different versions of the same person, and you end up wishing you hadn't asked. The memory plays strange tricks.

'As for the picture you are holding, it has a lot to do with the lighting. Remember, it was taken at night on an express train. The lighting, such as it was, rendered a quasi-romantic air which would be hard to replicate in a studio. It had a great deal to do with the arrangement of the shadows. I went to a great deal of trouble in finding, not only exactly the right angle but, if I say so myself, exactly the right moment when we were on a straight stretch of line. I was standing in the corridor with my back hard against the window. I remember the occupants of the next compartment gave me some very funny looks.'

It was the best he could manage on the spur of the moment.

'Pull the other leg,' said Doucette. 'It's got bells on it.

'That's what my father used to say,' she added hastily, as she caught sight of the expression on Aristide's face.

'I forgive you,' said Monsieur Pample-mousse. 'Did the girl tell you what time she would be back when she went out this morning?'

'No, but she did say we ought not to wait up,' said Doucette. 'She didn't know herself.'

'Suppose she can't get in?'

'I gave her the entry code for the building along with a spare key to our apartment in case she was very late back,' said Doucette. 'Old Lourbet hates being woken up. You know what he can be like if someone he doesn't know turns up out of the blue, especially if it's late at night. He usually pretends he didn't hear the bell.'

'You gave her a key to our apartment?' repeated Monsieur Pamplemousse. 'You didn't tell me that,' he added, accusingly.

'You didn't ask,' said Doucette. 'I gave it to her for the simple reason that if she was going to stay with us for any length of time she would most likely be coming and going a good deal, so she would be needing her own key.'

Monsieur Pamplemousse was only half satisfied with the answer, but he did his best to conceal the fact. He was wary of entrusting spare keys to other people at the best of times, however well he knew them. In the circumstances, lending them to a complete stranger was asking for trouble. Keys could be lost or stolen; and there was no knowing what might happen to them once they were out of their possession. Even if they were eventually returned, they could have been duplicated, and changing locks as a precautionary measure was a tedious business, particularly in an apartment block.

'It is possible, of course, that Caterina is up to her old tricks and whoever turned up was acting as a stand-in for her,' he said. 'I had been thinking the wearing of a red hat, which stands out in a crowd, was a deliberate act on her part, since that was what she was wearing on the last occasion. But it may simply have been a coincidence. It could even be that Caterina travelled on another train, or even flew to Paris. Red hats are part of the uniform of her old school and her stand-in might be an old classmate who is doing her a good turn.

'In which case I am the only one who could give the game away. Perhaps knowing that and never having met me, the girl panicked when she found out I was coming back.'

'How about the Director?' said Doucette. 'Wouldn't he recognise her?'

'To the best of my knowledge they have

never met,' said Monsieur Pamplemousse. 'His wife, Chantal, probably might have done at some point, seeing she is part of the family. But she is in Switzerland. The only mental picture of her Monsieur Leclercq has to go on are some shots I reeled off on her first trip when she was still in school uniform.'

'And you don't carry those around with you, of course,' said Doucette.

Ignoring the implication, Monsieur Pamplemousse shook his head. 'My wallet is full enough as it is.'

'Do you think it has anything to do with the fact that the fashion shows are in full swing?' suggested Doucette. 'If her father is so against the whole idea she may be trying to rustle up a few contacts on the quiet. She may even have stayed in Milan for a day or so while she had the chance and is planning on coming to Paris when she has finished.'

Monsieur Pamplemousse listened to Doucette's reasoning with only half an ear. In many respects it made sense, and it might well be the case, but hadn't Caterina's father put in a late plea for someone from *Le Guide* to meet her at the Gare de Lyon, and hadn't he suggested who that person should be? In the Director's eyes a suggestion from Caterina's father would be as good as a command.

Given that it sounded as though the request had been left until the last minute, Caterina wouldn't necessarily be aware of it, so she wouldn't have briefed her stand-in accordingly. Which would explain why the poor girl had panicked.

Whichever way you viewed the affair it seemed an unsatisfactory situation.

'It all comes back to Caterina,' he said. 'We won't know the answer until she puts in an appearance. And knowing her, that will be in her own good time.

'She has her sights firmly fixed on carving out a career for herself in the world of fashion, come what may. It is her goal in life and there is no getting away from it. The last thing she wants is to end up as what is known these days as a *"potiche"*: a beautiful and subservient wife dedicated to serving the selfish whims of a tyrannical husband.'

'She'll learn,' said Doucette. 'I shall tell her it isn't as bad as all that when I eventually do get to meet her.'

'Touché,' said Monsieur Pamplemousse. He knew when he was beaten. 'Aren't we lucky to have struck a happy medium.'

'Speak for yourself,' said Doucette dryly.

'Let me help with the washing up,' said Monsieur Pamplemousse hastily.

'It's all in the dishwasher,' said Doucette. 'I loaded the last of the plates while you were talking.'

'Well, at least allow me to turn it on,' said Monsieur Pamplemousse.

He bent down and peered at the controls.

'It helps if you make sure the door is properly closed,' said Doucette.

'They've thought of everything,' said Monsieur Pamplemousse.

Doucette joined him. 'Good old "they",' she said. 'What would we do without them?'

At which point, by mutual agreement, the subject was put on hold for the remainder of the day and only referred to briefly later that evening.

'What time did the girl get here last night?' asked Monsieur Pamplemousse.

'Soon after seven,' said Doucette. 'We chatted for a while and I showed her round the apartment. I asked her if she would like a bath after her journey. She said no, but went on to say she hadn't eaten for a while. That was when we got down to the cooking. I think she was impressed with all the food I've got in and it broke the ice. There's nothing quite like working together in a kitchen to let your hair down.'

'So what did you learn?'

'Not a lot,' admitted Doucette. 'She was much more interested hearing about you and your work.'

'How about baggage?'

'She said she had checked most of it in at the Gare de Lyon. She had all she needed for the time being in the shoulder bag she was carrying, which in turn was her cue for saying she felt like an early night, which at the time seemed a remarkably good idea.

'Now, having caught up on her sleep, the reverse is probably true and she is catching up on lost time, which means she can come back whenever she chooses. We don't have to wait up.'

Monsieur Pamplemousse considered the matter. It still went against the grain, but at least Pommes Frites, deprived of his usual sleeping space in the spare room, would be on guard to protect them. So bed it was.

'He's being very good about it,' said Doucette.

'He doesn't really have much choice,' said Monsieur Pamplemousse. 'Besides, for some reason his mind seems elsewhere.'

He would have given a lot to know exactly where it was, but knowing Pommes Frites of old he would have to wait. As with Caterina, all would be revealed in the fullness of time.

He'd more than once tried to find out what it was, but to no avail. His only hope was that if it was anything at all serious it wouldn't be too late.

'You needn't worry any more about the spare keys,' said Doucette, the next morning, when Monsieur Pamplemousse joined her for breakfast. 'Whoever the girl was, she didn't take them with her. She left them on the dressing table. Obviously she didn't intend coming back.'

'She might have told us,' said Monsieur Pamplemousse crossly. 'You're sure they're the right ones?'

'Positive,' said Doucette.

'May I see them for a moment?'

Doucette handed them over for Monsieur Pamplemousse to examine them minutely, but as far as he could see they were as clean as a whistle with no sign of any wax.

'You can't be too careful,' he said.

'I used them this morning when I went out early and bought some *croissants* for a change,' said Doucette.

'Ah!' said Monsieur Pamplemousse. At least things were looking up in one respect.

'I bought you some biscuits while I was at it,' said Doucette. 'That's another thing.

You've never told me you liked them, Aristide.'

'Finding out new things about one another over the years is one of the joys of marriage, Couscous,' said Monsieur Pamplemousse. 'Life might be very boring otherwise.'

'I shall make sure you are never without a full tin from now on,' said Doucette. '*If* there are any left. I tried one out on Pommes Frites and it went down a treat. I shall make sure you never have to ask again.

'Who could it have possibly been?' she continued. 'I lay awake worrying about it for ages last night. What with that and Pommes Frites pacing up and down, I didn't get more than a couple of hours' sleep, and you weren't much help, Aristide. Lying there like a log. You're sure it wasn't Caterina? At that age people can change almost overnight, girls especially. A touch of make-up can work wonders.'

'*Absolument!*' said Monsieur Pamplemousse. He reached for Doucette's photograph. 'It is in the eyes. This girl has brown eyes, Caterina's are the bluest of blue. A liquid blue.'

'It strikes me you ought to telephone Monsieur Leclercq and tell him what has happened,' said Doucette.

Monsieur Pamplemousse's heart sank. She was right, of course, but it was too early in the day to face yet another variation of Oscar Wilde's oft-quoted lines. Monsieur Leclercq would have a field day at his expense. It didn't bear thinking about.

'I suggest we finish our breakfast first,' he said.

'If nobody at all turns up what are we going to do with all this food?' said Doucette.

'Eat it, I suppose,' said Monsieur Pamplemousse gloomily. 'We could ask a few friends in and throw an all-Italian party. Perhaps your acquaintance at Bon Marché will have a few ideas. He didn't seem short of them. What was his name ... Giovanni? You could ask him along too.'

He hastily changed the subject.

'I wonder why?' he said.

'Why?'

'Why the girl was here at all. She must have had a good reason; both for coming in the first place and then for leaving so abruptly. Did she say anything about not being met?'

'Not specifically. But I said how much you had enjoyed her company on the train when she paid her first visit to Paris.'

And afterwards, thought Monsieur Pamplemousse, when he had turned up at the

158

eleventh hour and saved Caterina and a whole coachload of her friends from public disgrace and a possible prison sentence. The event had been hushed up at the time, and never referred to again as far as he knew. He hoped the girl would pass Doucette's reaction on to the real Caterina.

'I don't know quite why, but I assumed she must have rung the Director first and he gave her our address...' said Doucette. 'I suppose she must have forgotten it.'

So far, so true, thought Monsieur Pamplemousse. The Director's reaction would have been par for the course. As far as he knew Monsieur Leclercq and Caterina had never actually met each other so, like a boxer, he would have been thinking on his feet.

In which case, it was definitely himself the girl hadn't wanted to meet. Presumably because that would have given the game away. No wonder she had looked bothered when Doucette took her picture.

And if that were the case, what was the name of the game?

'Talking of parties,' said Doucette. 'Your old friend Jacques phoned while you were out yesterday morning. He said perhaps you could ring him back when you had a moment.

'I asked him if it was anything important, and he said not really. It was simply a matter of life and death.'

Monsieur Pamplemousse gave a sigh as he reached for the phone and dialled a number. One of these days Jacques' sense of humour was going to be the death of him.

He didn't have long to wait.

'That little skirmish on the canal St Martin towpath you mentioned the last time we spoke...'

It wasn't so little, thought Monsieur Pamplemousse. But carry on. All these things are relative, especially given the location.

'Sorry I took such a long time over it,' said Jacques, 'but it happened a week or so before the date you gave me. Anyway, whoever it was used a spring-loaded staple gun. The kind upholsterers use for laying extra-thick carpet. It's relatively silent compared with a gun. You can creep up behind people and catch them unawares. Which must have been precisely what happened, according to the medical report. It doesn't sound like the Mafia. They like to do it up front.'

'You think it was plain robbery that went wrong?'

'Robbery with intent to kill,' said Jacques. 'That would be my guess, and that was the conclusion of the report. His wallet was missing. Probably the day's takings or maybe the week's. In which case he could have been loaded.

'Strange thing ... the victim was wearing a topcoat and you won't believe this but in one of the pockets there was a large steak. Or what looked like a steak. When they took a closer look it was made of plastic. It sounds like he'd been working a scam of some kind.'

'I believe you,' said Monsieur Pamplemousse. 'Just one thing ... spare me the gory details, but how do you know the weapon was a stapler?'

'The body had an obituary notice attached,' said Jacques. 'Also, we sent the divers in and they recovered it.'

'It was my turn to ask a silly question,' said Monsieur Pamplemousse.

'Enjoy your lunch,' said Jacques.

'Cheer up, Couscous,' said Monsieur Pamplemousse, as he caught the look on her face. 'It isn't the end of the world.'

'Speak for yourself, Aristide,' said Doucette. 'But I couldn't help overhearing your end of the conversation. It strikes me there must be those who might not be too happy with your summing up.'

'Paraphrasing Abraham Lincoln,' said

Monsieur Pamplemousse. 'You can't please all the people all the time.

'Talking of which, Monsieur Leclercq was still going on about my missing the train at the Gare de Lyon when I left him. He has no idea what the station was like before all the changes took place, so it's a waste of time trying to explain what went wrong.'

'What did happen there?' asked Doucette. 'I can't begin to picture what it must be like now.'

'I'll show you if you like, Couscous,' said Monsieur Pamplemousse, relieved to have got away from the subject of what happened on the canal St Martin.

Removing the SD card from his own camera, he inserted it into the television. If he wasn't careful he could end up as a tame projectionist going through his vast store of digital photographs. That said, he couldn't wait to see what his current shots of the station were like on the big screen.

'It doesn't look any different to me,' said Doucette, as the first one taken from the stairs outside the restaurant filled the screen.

'It isn't,' said Monsieur Pamplemousse. 'Apart from the fact that the train I was supposed to meet doesn't arrive there any more.'

Lingering for a moment or two over the

next shot of the empty platforms devoid of humanity to emphasise his point, he wished now he had stopped to take more pictures of the route between that part of the station and the newly completed Hall 2. A few crowd shots on the way, along with close-ups of other befuddled individuals like himself, would have painted a better picture of the whole. But then, his mind had been on other things.

The picture of an empty *Quai 7* was equally dispiriting, and running through the shots he had taken at random of the hall itself in the hope of coming across Caterina lurking somewhere in the vast area only made him realise what a forlorn exercise it had been. At that time of the year everyone was wearing black and it reminded him of a Lowry painting. Doucette was right about one thing. If the girl had been wearing a red hat she would have stood out like a sore thumb.

He was about to say as much when she intervened. 'Could you go back one?'

Monsieur Pamplemousse obliged. 'Don't tell me you've seen someone you know? They all look the same to me.'

Doucette crossed to the television and pointed to a figure in a long black overcoat standing to one side of a small kiosk. 'It isn't anyone I know,' she said. 'But he came past our block the day afterwards. If that isn't a coincidence, I don't know what is. I could have sworn he looked up towards our floor.

'I know what you're thinking,' she continued. 'But it wasn't just him, it was the dog he had with him on both occasions. A little black thing. Very self-possessed it was, with a lovely little beard and his tail straight up in the air as though he owned the world.

'I looked him up in your dog book. It's what's known as a Scottie. You see their picture on the side of Scotch whisky bottles. Do you think it's an omen?'

Monsieur Pamplemousse didn't believe in coincidences, or omens come to that, but Doucette was clearly so excited by the whole thing he hadn't the heart to dampen her enthusiasm by saying the man might simply have been looking up to see if it was going to rain.

'Let me know if it happens again,' he said, removing the card. 'I'll have a word with Pommes Frites and see what he thinks.'

CHAPTER SEVEN

'I may only be a *femme au foyer*, Aristide,' said Doucette, 'but there is something underhand going on, and it gives me a nasty feeling. I still can't come to terms with that girl coming and going like she did. She may have been a nice person, but in a way that only makes it worse. Somehow the whole thing is far more upsetting than a burglary. A simple breaking and entering I could cope with, but what has happened is an intrusion of our territory and it's hard to explain, but I feel it has been violated.'

'Ah,' said Aristide. *'Le terroir!* To a French man or woman that is the most sacred thing of all. I do sympathise.'

'Now, as far as I can gather,' said Doucette, 'it is somehow connected with a murder on the canal St Martin.'

'Something is rotten in the state of Denmark,' agreed Monsieur Pamplemousse, 'and it grieves me not knowing what it is. As for the unfortunate affair on the banks of the canal St Martin, the least said the better.'

Doucette stared at him. 'Unfortunate?' she said. 'There speaks an ex-member of the Paris Sûreté. Sometimes I wonder how I came to marry you.'

'You can't help being a person of taste and discernment,' said Monsieur Pamplemousse.

'What do you see when you look in the mirror, Aristide?' asked Doucette.

'Someone else of taste and discernment,' said Monsieur Pamplemousse. 'Tall, dark, handsome...'

'I must give it a good clean,' said Doucette.

'It's like I have just said,' responded Monsieur Pamplemousse. 'Abraham Lincoln was absolutely right. You can't fool all the people all the time. Is it my fault you see something totally different? Which reminds me... How about Pommes Frites? How did he behave towards the girl?'

'He wasn't exactly on his best behaviour,' said Doucette. 'He was in a funny mood.'

'Then it definitely couldn't have been Caterina,' said Monsieur Pamplemousse. 'He never forgets a face and they got on well together.'

'He did cheer up a bit when she received a telephone call.'

'On our phone? You didn't tell me that.'

'No,' said Doucette. 'She had a mobile and

the call came through soon after she arrived. Don't ask me why, but I assumed it was Monsieur Leclercq making sure she had arrived safely. It was short, sharp, and to the point.'

'That doesn't sound like the Director,' said Monsieur Pamplemousse.

'Anyway, it certainly got Pommes Frites going. It was one of those phones that vibrates instead of ringing and I don't think he had ever come across one before. He couldn't wait to get a closer look at it. It seemed to break the ice. His tail was beating time like nobody's business.

'Another funny thing happened soon afterwards. He pushed the door to your den open and went inside. I peeped in to see what he wanted and he was peering at your mobile, but it was on the charger. He looked most disappointed.'

Monsieur Pamplemousse fell silent for a moment or two. Clearly there must be a connection with whatever problem was occupying Pommes Frites' mind, but for the moment he couldn't think what it could possibly be.

Doucette brought him back down to earth.

'Have you ever met Uncle Caputo?' she

asked. 'The very name gives me the shivers.'

'No,' said Monsieur Pamplemousse. 'And I have no wish to. I might like him and life is complicated enough as it is. Besides, it is only a nickname. My understanding is that apart from his connections with the Cosa Nostra, he is a pillar of Sicilian society.

'As for you calling yourself a mere housewife, Doucette, I have never heard such nonsense. There is nothing mere about being a housewife.'

'And there is nothing mere about the Cosa Nostra,' said Doucette. 'It's really only another name for the Mafia.'

'On the contrary,' said Monsieur Pamplemousse. 'It's the other way round. The Cosa Nostra came first. Roughly translated it means "our thing". Way back in the early nineteenth century, when feudalism was giving way to more enlightened thinking, Sicily is where it all began. Small groups known as "families" got together in order to offer protection to those who needed it most: peasants holding out against the big landowners who were trying to grind them into the dirt, and on the other side of the coin the nobility, who were living in constant fear of the peasants rising up. In effect the Cosa Nostra took over from the state in enforcing the law at a time when the powers that be couldn't cope with the situation.

'Unfortunately, what started off with the best of intentions by men of honour gradually deteriorated into a money-making exercise *per se*. In fact, from that time on it not only became a core activity of the Cosa Nostra, but something of a racket which in time turned into a necessity if large companies were to survive at all. It is said that even today around seventy per cent of businesses on the island still seek protection for fear of what might happen if they didn't play ball.'

'Protection from what?' Doucette set to work replenishing the coffee.

'Unplanned disasters,' said Monsieur Pamplemousse. 'At its most basic a member of the mob goes into a thriving restaurant and after complimenting the owner on a meal he has just enjoyed, casually remarks wouldn't it be a shame if one day a customer found the remains of a dead rat in his soup? That simple statement is followed by an offer to make sure it never comes to pass. At a price, of course.'

'And they don't call the police?'

'Only a true Sicilian can be a member of the Cosa Nostra,' said Monsieur Pamplemousse. 'And they mean what they say. It is a variation of making someone an offer they can't refuse. The plus side in their case is that protection comes with a capital *P*. Nothing is ever written down on paper, but they never go back on a promise.'

Doucette poured the coffee. 'Biscuits?'

Monsieur Pamplemousse shook his head. 'Not just after breakfast. I might grow tired of them. Sometimes I can go for hours without one.'

'And the worldwide Mafia as a whole,' said Doucette. 'What about that?'

'Towards the end of the nineteeth century Italy annexed Sicily and set about reshaping the country. A great many of the Cosa Nostra fled to America and set up shop there. Prohibition was in full swing with its speakeasies. From then on what was nicknamed the Mafia became a branch of general crime attracting other nationalities seeking a new life in America to its ranks. First of all it was the Irish, then the Jews, followed by the Italians. But as I said, it all began in Sicily. As for Italy, it became overrun by the Neapolitan Camorra. But that's another story.

'In the meantime the authorities in Sicily thought they had got the upper hand, but the Second World War changed all that. Following the devastation wrought by the Allies when around half a million of them invaded the island in order to reclaim it, the Cosa Nostra came into its own again, and later received a further fillip when the heroin that had previously gone to America via Marseilles was diverted to make the journey via Palermo. They were living in clover again.'

'And they are allowed to get away with it?'

'As someone once put it: "All power corrupts. Absolute power corrupts absolutely." It's a constant battle and the Mafia have a powerful weapon on their side; it is called Omertà; the code of silence.

'They don't keep records. No member introduces himself to another member he doesn't know personally. It has to be done through a third person.

'Everything is geared to secrecy. Also, it has to be remembered that the Cosa Nostra isn't a single body but more an association of "families", each of which rules over its own territory independent of the others.

'Some people who are not fully fledged members but work for families on and off are even entering the tourism business, renting out lonely properties which once belonged to the old-time bosses for people who want to get away from it all.'

'Is that where Uncle Caputo comes in?'

'It wouldn't surprise me,' said Monsieur Pamplemousse.

'I still don't like it,' said Doucette. 'I'm beginning to feel as though I have lost control of everything around me. It's like being caught up in a giant spider's web.'

'There is one big difference,' said Monsieur Pamplemousse. 'You have nothing to fear from a spider's web. They are there to act as a trap to catch food. No less and no more.'

'Who says?' demanded Doucette.

'Jacques for one,' said Monsieur Pamplemousse. 'I remember making the same comment as you have just made some years back when we were working on a case together and he shot me down in flames. He maintains that even the actual construction of the web is exactly the same as has always been. The only variable is where it lands.

'As for where they begin and where they end, I know someone much nearer home who can tell you all you need to know on the subject. Ron Barnaud was sounding off about it only the other day in the common room... Apparently there are some in the room where he is working.'

He picked up the telephone receiver. Anything to soothe Doucette's fears.

'I'll see if I can get hold of him. He's our tame scientist. Besides, he owes me one for not telling me about all the changes at the Gare de Lyon. *If* he knew himself, of course.' Holding the receiver away from his ear, he pressed the enhanced hearing button so that Doucette could join in if she wanted to.

'My understanding,' said Barnaud, when Monsieur Pamplemousse asked the question, 'has always been that it is largely a matter of luck. An arachnid simply releases a strand of sticky thread of a suitable length depending on its own size and then lets go of it.

'Propelled by any light breeze which happens to be present, the thread floats away and attaches itself to the first thing it meets. If where it has landed is to the spider's liking, it makes its way along the thread, reinforcing it as it goes. The next step is to set to work manufacturing what amounts to a Y-shaped attachment, the top ends of which hang from either end of the original thread.

'If you can picture it, the centre point of the Y becomes the centre point of the finished web and the three separate parts of the Y form the first of a set of radii which eventually are held in place by the four sides of a rough square.

'Once that is done to its satisfaction it sits

173

in the middle of the web to await the arrival of its prey. They have been doing it that way for over 100 million years and they are not going to change now.'

For some reason Barnaud sounded unusually detached. In all probability he was hard at work on his app and didn't welcome any diversions.

'And if it doesn't catch anything?'

'It goes through the same process all over again somewhere else. Why do you ask?'

'My wife posed the question,' said Monsieur Pamplemousse. 'She suffers from arachnophobia.'

'Tell him being a spider is even worse than being a housewife,' hissed Doucette. 'All that work and nothing to show for it at the end of the day wouldn't suit me at all. I would sooner be Pommes Frites. If anyone knows the answer to our current problem he clearly does, but he can't tell us, more's the pity.'

'Give him time,' said Monsieur Pamplemousse. 'He'll find a way.'

Relieved that Doucette showed signs of recovering from her attack of the blues, as though a dark cloud overhead had passed on its way, he repeated what she had said and having received no response, thanked

Barnaud for his trouble and replaced the receiver.

'What do you mean I "suffer from arachnophobia"?' said Doucette. 'I may not like spiders, but I don't have a phobia about them.'

'Barnaud can be very nosy when he likes, and he's not as clever as he thinks he is,' said Monsieur Pamplemousse, who was still smarting over his experience at the Gare de Lyon. 'He wants to know everything. It's none of his business why you asked... Anyway, let's get back to basics...'

'Perhaps we could start by making a list of all the things you know for certain,' suggested Doucette.

'In my case it would be very short,' said Monsieur Pamplemousse. 'I suggest we set to work on all the things we *think* we know for certain, but don't necessarily.'

'Such as?'

'Who really killed the owner of the restaurant? Or had him killed? And why?'

'You think it had nothing to do with Uncle Caputo?'

'According to Jacques it happened some time before we thought it did and anyway it didn't sound like a Mafia job. It was too amateurish and when it comes to killing someone, the Mafia don't usually subcontract. If they do, the person doing the dirty work for them is almost certain to be eliminated shortly after for safety's sake. But that doesn't mean to say *Le Guide* isn't involved in some way.'

'What else don't you know for sure?' asked Doucette.

'The date on the email Monsieur Leclercq received from the member of the Club des Cent. That would narrow things down a bit. I don't recall seeing one.'

'We don't know how he received the message about Caterina's visit to Paris. There are so many different ways of communicating these days. Emails; phone text; we are spoilt for choice. How do we know the Director even spoke to Caterina's father, still less that it was he who suggested I should meet her?'

'But, surely,' began Doucette, 'even Monsieur Leclercq isn't that gullible.'

'Monsieur Leclercq's mind is currently taken up with two things,' said Monsieur Pamplemousse. 'The loss of a giant truffle which happens to be the property of his wife's uncle...' He paused. 'Come to that I don't even know how he received it in the first place.'

'And the other thing that is so important?'

'Overriding everything is the fact that *Le*

Guide is in the final stages of completion for the coming year. As always, everything else takes a back seat. He spent most of yesterday going through it with Véronique making sure everything was as it should be; not simply those restaurants scheduled to go up in the world, but those that are going down. 'What makes accuracy doubly important this year is the fact that if all goes well he has another project up his sleeve.'

One way and another Monsieur Pamplemousse managed to put off calling the office until halfway through the morning, and when he finally got through it was brief and to the point, or so it seemed to Doucette.

'You look worried, Aristide,' she said.

'Not so much worried,' said Monsieur Pamplemousse, 'as puzzled. Bemused, to tell you the truth.

'The girl's been in to see the Director already. Apparently she said nothing about her stay here. She simply picked up the truffle and left.'

'Just like that?'

'She said she was doing it on behalf of her father and couldn't stop ... she was late for an important engagement. While she was there she had a call on her mobile and that did the trick. In her haste to make a quick getaway she dropped it and before anyone had a chance to argue with her she had disappeared.'

'Nobody questioned her or asked for any proof of identity?'

'Apparently not,' said Monsieur Pamplemousse. 'Véronique has never met the real Caterina either. If I may borrow that photograph you took of her I can email it through and see what she says.'

Five minutes later and the result was in his hands. He read her response out loud. '"Superb. Monsieur Leclercq's niece is real poppet. Should make good cover for the staff magazine. Any chance of two postcards for luck?? Véronique."'

'Fronting *L'Escargot* indeed!' Monsieur Pamplemousse signalled Pommes Frites to his side. 'If you ask me it's high time we paid another visit to the office.'

'One up for the humble email,' said Doucette.

'Don't be late back tonight,' she called. 'I thought I would try my hand at stuffed peppers, Neapolitan style ... Giovanni gave me the recipe.'

'It must be good then,' said Monsieur Pamplemousse, as he beat a hasty retreat.

He wasn't far from the office, approaching it via the Pont Alexandre III – setting for the romantic finale of Woody Allen's *Midnight in Paris* – when a feeling of *déjà vu* came over him.

If questioned, he would have been hard put to say why. Perhaps it was the memory of the rainswept bridge at midnight filling the screen. Then again, perhaps not. There were times when everywhere in Paris felt like a film set.

Having started out fully intending to reach the office as fast as he could, he slowed down and tucked himself in behind a slow-moving excursion bus heading towards Les Invalides and one or other of its three vast museums. Perhaps, given the time of year and the fact that it was off-season for tourists, it would take in all three for the benefit of the few passengers huddled on the open top deck, with the Dome and Napoleon's tomb thrown in for good measure. The possibility didn't do anything for his *joie de vivre* which was getting lower by the minute.

His remark to Doucette regarding the state of Denmark had been a throwaway comment made on the spur of the moment to soothe her obvious fears. Now he wasn't so sure. Pre-publication time at *Le Guide* was rarely without its dramas, real and/or imagined. A single typo or misspelling of a word passed over during countless readings and rereadings during the proof stage would stand out like the proverbial sore thumb once it appeared in the final publication and there was no going back.

Not that he had experienced such an occurrence, but there was a first time for everything. Now he was on his own he began to see things in a more analytical light. Everything suddenly looked more serious and once a publication was in the shops there was nothing you could do about it. The damage was done.

His mind went back a few years. Heaven forbid it should be another case of sabotage on the very eve of publication, as had happened when the disk on the main computer was hijacked. The object then had been revenge and it had very nearly succeeded.

On that occasion they had been a hair's breadth away from awarding the Golden Stock Pot lid for the best restaurant in all France to the Wun Pooh – a Chinese takeaway in Dieppe, the consequence of which would have been their becoming the laughing stock of gourmets everywhere. Michelin and Pudlo would have been rolling in the aisles.

At the other extreme, remove a Stock Pot or two from a flourishing establishment without very good reason, and the lawyers would have a field day.

Buying a few more minutes of time before reaching his destination, he took a left turn and circumnavigated the Esplanade des Invalides in order to approach the rue Fabert from the opposite direction to the one he usually took.

Sensing his master's change of mood, and coupling it with the departure from their normal routine, Pommes Frites also suffered a sea change in his demeanour as he gazed out of the car window. He'd heard the word truffle mentioned before they came out. In fact, as far as he could make out the giant truffle was the main reason why they were going into the office. Given the power of speech he could have told them a thing or two.

If only he could find a way of explaining what he knew to be a fact, he felt sure it would make all the difference.

He would find a way, *must* find a way of communicating it. But for the time being he had to content himself with a supporting role as he followed his master into Monsieur Leclercq's office where, to the surprise of both of them, there was a small gathering of familiar faces.

'Pamplemousse...' The Director rose to his feet, hand outstretched, as they entered. 'And Pommes Frites. This *is* a pleasant surprise.'

'We came as soon as we heard the news,' said Monsieur Pamplemousse.

The Director continued the wave of his hand to take in the other members of the group: his secretary, Véronique; Madame Grante, the Head of Accounts; and Mlle Ranier, the Head of Reception.

'I am just apprising these key members of my staff as to the unhappy event that has taken place. Véronique was here at the time to witness it, of course, and although I am aware that what has happened is of no great moment and we have nothing to worry about, given the parties involved and the nature of the happening, not to mention the salient fact that we are almost on the eve of publication and just prior to a major event yet to be announced, I feel it is incumbent on me to make sure everyone in this room is in the picture and fully conversant with the situation, lest there be any other last-minute untoward distractions which will divert attention away from the main reason for our

182

very existence.'

When he was 'on song' Monsieur Leclercq wasn't in the habit of making do with one word when he could seize the opportunity of fitting in four or five more. It was thirsty work and he poured himself a liberal glass of water.

'You are all free to ask questions,' he said, when he had finished

'May I ask,' said Madame Grante, 'what *is* the main event?'

'I am afraid not,' said Monsieur Leclercq firmly. 'It will be announced shortly.'

'I simply wished to be fully conversant with all that is going on,' said Madame Grante stiffly.

'You will be, dear lady,' said the Director. 'You will be any day now. I have yet to receive the all-clear from a certain person.'

Monsieur Pamplemousse seized the opportunity to ask Mlle Ranier a question.

'No,' said the Head of Reception. 'The truffle didn't arrive in the mail. It was delivered by a courier to the main desk. It was contained in a small parcel labelled URGENT – STRICTLY PRIVATE, and addressed to the Director.

'Nobody saw the person who delivered it,' she added. 'But that is what *must* have happened. These things don't appear as though by magic.'

'And the note that came with it?' Monsieur Pamplemousse ignored the implied reproof. 'There was nothing to say how the truffle was to be returned. Only that it should be?'

Monsieur Leclercq reaffirmed that fact and everyone else in the room waited patiently while he searched for the original note in a sheaf of papers on his desk.

'He simply said he was seeking an expert opinion on its validity.'

'That was all?'

'My wife's uncle is a man of few words,' said Monsieur Leclercq. 'Had he intended me to keep the truffle he would have said so. When I heard Caterina was planning a visit to Paris I assumed she would be taking charge of it and I had Véronique make sure it was ready for collection.'

'Ah,' said Monsieur Pamplemousse. 'That brings me to the reason why I am here.'

Reaching inside his jacket he produced Doucette's photograph and held it up for everyone to see. 'I simply ask to make sure all of those who were present at the time are agreed that this is the girl who collected it.'

'I spoke to her when she arrived,' said Mlle Ranier. 'She couldn't have been nicer.'

'Utterly charming,' agreed the Director. 'She spoke very highly of your wife, Pamplemousse. They got on like a house on fire.

'We only wish we could have seen more of her, but she was in a terrible hurry as it was. The phone message I mentioned when we spoke, whoever it was from, and whatever it was about, really clinched matters. She went as white as a sheet, and having dropped the mobile in her haste, made a dash for it.' He pointed to the spot on the floor where it had landed.

'She didn't even sign herself out, let alone have time to wave goodbye,' said Mlle Ranier. 'The girls on the front desk were very upset.'

Monsieur Pamplemousse lowered the photograph, and it was only then that he delivered his bombshell. 'I ask,' he said, 'because the girl in this picture is not Caterina.'

His words had the desired effect.

Madame Grante suffered an immediate attack of palpitations and having produced a phial of smelling salts from her handbag and taken a good sniff, she offered it around, but there were no takers.

'Can this be, Pamplemousse?' asked Monsieur Leclercq. 'Are you absolutely positive?'

'Never more certain,' said Monsieur Pam-

185

plemousse. 'I very much fear we are the victims of a plot.' He was about to add more when a faint buzzing sound came from the object on the floor.

For a second or two, as it began to move slowly along the carpet propelled by the vibrations within, all those present stood rooted to the spot until Pommes Frites made a dive for it and having picked the instrument up in his jaws hurried across the room.

Monsieur Pamplemousse dashed after him, shouting *asseyez-vous* as he went, but for once he called in vain.

Pommes Frites beat his master to Monsieur Leclercq's waste bucket by a whisker, and as he leant over the side he opened his mouth to relieve himself of the load. There was a loud splash and the buzzing ceased.

Seeing a stream of bubbles rising to the surface, Monsieur Pamplemousse flung off his jacket, rolled up the shirtsleeve of his right arm, and seconds later withdrew a dripping mobile.

He held it up to his ear, but there was nothing. 'Give it time,' he said, stifling his embarrassment. 'I'm sure it will dry out.'

'Unfortunately time is not on our side, Pamplemousse,' said Monsieur Leclercq severely. 'It could well be that we shall never know who was making the call until it is too late and it may well have been serious.'

'I told Hortense not to fill the bin with water,' said Véronique, coming to Pommes Frites' rescue in the silence that followed. 'But she would have her way. She said it needed a good clean-out after what happened before.'

'I'm sure he meant well,' said Monsieur Pamplemousse.

Madame Grante gave vent to another loud sniff which was another way of saying: 'Catch Joey doing a thing like that!'

'Perhaps,' said Monsieur Leclercq, 'Pommes Frites would be better employed if he made use of his olfactory powers to find a replacement truffle for us. I think it is the least he can do in the circumstances. A real one, even if it is only half the size of the original, would be some recompense to Chantal's uncle.'

'It isn't as straightforward as that, I fear,' said Monsieur Pamplemousse. 'It is already getting late in the year for anything anywhere near the size we would need.

'As for the original *faux* truffle... Had it not already been collected, I was going to suggest it could perhaps be airmailed back to Japan. It wasn't damaged beyond repair.

All it really needed was a good clean-up.'

He could have said more, but glancing down he changed his mind.

Pommes Frites' eyes looked so full of joy it was impossible to be cross with him. As if to underline matters, instead of his tail wagging to and fro as it normally did when he was pleased about something, it was performing definite arcs in the air behind him: a classic sign if ever there was one that not only was he over the moon with his handiwork, he wanted to share the outcome with his master.

In many respects it was reminiscent of his behaviour with the original truffle, and since it meant nothing more than that to Monsieur Pamplemousse, for the time being at least, there was nothing more he could add to it.

CHAPTER EIGHT

'Where *have* you been, Aristide?' said Doucette when they eventually reached home. 'The stuffed peppers must be like bullets by now.'

'We could go out to eat,' said Monsieur Pamplemousse. 'There's that restaurant in rue des Martyrs you wanted to try ... Le Miroir. It should be listed in next year's guide. It's been put forward as a candidate for a wrought-iron table and chair. That will put it a step or two above a bar stool.'

'And the rue des Martyrs is several steps above where I want to go at this time of night,' said Doucette. 'Besides, it's probably packed out by now. If Pommes Frites can manage bones, he should be able to get his teeth into my peppers. I can rustle up something else for us. Heaven knows we've enough things that need using up.

'I had been toying with trying my hand at making a mozzarella and basil pizza, but I've given up on the idea.'

'That doesn't sound like you,' said Monsieur Pamplemousse. 'Giving up, I mean.'

'There comes a time,' said Doucette. 'You are right about one thing, Aristide. In certain respects Italian cuisine hasn't changed in a hundred years. To start with, according to my book, in order to make a satisfactory Neapolitan pizza you need a wood-fired oven. Nothing else will do. It requires that amount of heat.'

She held up a hand. 'I know what you're

going say, but where would we put it? Knowing you, it would probably come gift-wrapped and I have enough problems getting rid of all the waste paper as it is.

'Secondly, the flour used to make the base needs to be as fine as it can possibly be – almost like talcum powder, and when you have made the dough it should be allowed to rise slowly to room temperature for twenty-four hours...'

'I do see your problem, Couscous,' said Monsieur Pamplemousse. 'But if it's of any consolation, and it grieves me to say it, I'm not sure Pommes Frites deserves anything at all. We are not exactly popular back at the works.'

He related at length what had taken place in the Director's office.

'That sounds very unlike him too,' said Doucette.

'I think he was trying to tell me something and I feel I've let him down,' said Monsieur Pamplemousse. 'It was one of those phones that vibrates rather than rings. I don't know if he thought it was something alive or not.'

'Perhaps it has to do with that particular telephone,' said Doucette. 'If you remember, I told you it had a similar effect on him when it went off while she was here.

'Incidentally, that man with the dog came past again while you were out. You could set your watch by them. *Huit heures précises, midi, et dix-huit.* He waited around a bit longer than usual reading a hand-held while his dog had a biscuit or two. They had come up the hill and his little legs were going so fast you could hardly see them. I think he was in need of some sustenance.

'Anyway, I want to hear about all the other things going on at the office and we can't talk if we're in a crowded restaurant.

'What *is* happening to *Le Guide?* When I tried to phone you the girl on the switchboard wanted to know my date of birth and my mother's maiden name. She even asked me where I was born. Anyone would think I was wanting to set up an account with American Express. She ought to be able to recognise my voice by now.'

'She was only obeying my instructions, Couscous.'

'*Your* instructions?'

'History is repeating itself,' said Monsieur Pamplemousse. 'The Director has promoted me to the post of *Chef de Sécurité.* CS for short, but as the old saying goes "Not for long", I hope.'

'And you said yes like you did the last

time?' said Doucette. 'Acting unpaid I pre-sume.'

'I could hardly say no,' said Monsieur Pamplemousse. 'You know how Monsieur Leclercq is about any publicity, especially at this time of the year. He's like the proverbial cat on hot bricks. The media would have a field day if he brought the police in, or any big security organisation come to that, and at least I still have my unofficial connections with the Sûreté. Jacques is as good as his word. He won't let it go any further.'

'That only answers the first half of my question,' said Doucette.

'We are all in it together,' said Monsieur Pamplemousse. 'Besides it's only temporary. I don't need to be paid for it. In the mean-time, for better or worse, I have put the whole organisation on *alerte rouge*. I am not too popular as it is and I don't want to make it any worse by getting paid extra for it into the bargain.'

'What happened to the Director's so called "three As rule"?' said Doucette. *'Action; Accord;Anonymat.* As far as I can see they are all conspicuous by their absence. Apart from anything else, I thought he always had a routine check by an outside company before you went to press.'

'I'm taking care of the *action*,' said Monsieur Pamplemousse. 'I'm hoping *"accord"* will come as a matter of course and as anonymously as possible if we all keep our mouths shut.

'As for the routine check, as ever it's centred on Monsieur Leclercq's office and it's not exactly on the cutting edge of today's security. They check behind the Founder's portrait to make sure there isn't a hidden microphone planted there, "as happened when the Russians presented the American Ambassador with the Great Seal of the United States after the last war", which rather says it all.

'We have moved on in the world of electronic surveillance since then.

'They check the telephone handsets and all the power points to make sure there are no hidden devices. There is a lot of empty space in the average handset. The covers can be removed in a matter of seconds and they are just crying out for a 'drop-in' bug, which nowadays can be powered by the telephone itself.

'They then go outside on the balcony to make sure there are no directional microphones within range, while the Director pays a visit to his drinks cupboard to fuel their enthusiasm. It is part of an annual ritual and is a social occasion.'

'They ought to look in the drinks cupboard for a start,' said Doucette.

Monsieur Pamplemousse went on to enumerate other possible suspect areas, but before he had finished their own phone began to ring.

'Don't worry about answering it,' said Doucette. 'It's probably another "hang-up". I've had three already since you left for the office.'

'Have you now?' Monsieur Pamplemousse registered the fact without further comment. He filed it alongside the man with the dog. He could do without both of them.

It wasn't the moment to suggest his wife might like to stay with her sister Agathe in Melun until everything had blown over, so he put that on 'hold' as well.

'I suppose you'll be bundling me off to my sister in Melun for safekeeping next,' said Doucette. 'If it's anything like last time, I shan't see you for goodness knows how long. I love her very dearly, but two days is more than enough. As for her cooking...'

'It wouldn't be for long,' said Monsieur Pamplemousse. 'I'll make sure of that. Besides there isn't that much time left before publication day.'

'Perhaps Pommes Frites could keep guard while you're busy at the office this time?' suggested Doucette.

'I think not, Couscous. Although I say it myself, he is a typical bloodhound. His nerve centre resides in the end of his nose, which is why it's bigger than most other dogs. Even his ears are overlarge on purpose, not because they are an aid to his hearing, but simply so that with a couple of shakes of his head he can direct any scent in the right direction. They are also blessed with a phenomenal memory. He wouldn't think twice about following a week-old trail to Kathmandu and back if required, and he would guard you with his life if he thought someone was attacking you. One scream and he would be right by your side.

'But he is like all bloodhounds. In his heart of hearts he is also meek and mild and everybody's friend, so he is just as likely to give any intruder a welcoming lick before passing judgement.'

Doucette changed the subject. 'Did you find out the answers to all your questions, Aristide?'

'It was much as I expected it to be,' said Monsieur Pamplemousse. 'Véronique is right when she says communication has gone completely over the top. There is so much information flying around, a great deal of it of no use to anyone, or none of their business anyway. The atmosphere must be getting weighed down by it all. It's no wonder the weather has been so bad lately.

'We live in a world where we see people communicating with each other all the time. They roam the streets with what looks like an umbilical cord that has been split down the middle, so that once they have disentangled all the knitting, both ends can be attached, one to each ear.

'Or else they wander past you, seemingly talking to themselves in a loud voice, utterly oblivious to the fact that all those around them can hear everything they say.

'Worst of all are the ones who get off a train or bus and immediately stop dead in their tracks in order to type in a text message telling someone, who probably lives just round the corner, they are on their way.

'Even cinemas suffer little pockets of light as half the audience take it into their heads to send and receive text messages, oblivious to the fact that they are spoiling the film for others.

'As for emails. They are a wonderful invention; ideal for sending a round-robin message

196

when it's a matter of conveying some piece of general information that doesn't require immediate action. But they, too, have their downside. The worst aspect is the fact that people who send you an individual message invariably expect an instant reply. The days of being able to sleep on a problem and come up with a measured response the next morning are long since past; more's the pity – the world has speeded up enough already. And that's without Facebook and Twitter and goodness knows what else yet to be invented. It's never-ending, and when it comes to the begetter of it all – the humble telephone – I fear women are the worst offenders.'

'Have you quite finished?' asked Doucette.

'It was the same with the arrangements for Caterina,' continued Monsieur Pamplemousse, totally undeterred by the interruption. 'They were either messages that had been emailed or sent by text. I can't find a single concrete occasion when there is proof positive of there having been an actual voice-to-voice conversation.

'Interestingly, the message the Director received from the Club des Cent, which was really at the start of everything, appears to have been undated. That fact seems to have gone unnoticed at the time, so I told him his wife could rest easily from now on when she gets back from Switzerland. The restaurant owner's murder wasn't as a result of what she misguidedly told her Uncle Rocco.'

'How about the one asking for Caterina to be met at the Gare de Lyon and nominating you for the job?'

'The first part was short, to the point and unsigned, so it might have been from anyone.

'As for choosing me for the task, Monsieur Leclercq unwittingly admitted it was his idea. "I know Chantal's uncle," he said. "It was what he would have liked most of all, so I did it to please him."'

'And you didn't query the fact?' said Doucette.

'I did,' said Monsieur Pamplemousse, 'and do you know what he said? "You don't query messages from Madame Leclercq's uncle, Pamplemousse."

'In short, he had already convinced himself that it was Uncle Rocco who had come up with the idea, not himself.

'Anyway, enough of all that. First things first. I must get on to Jacques and see if he has any ideas about tracking down the girl. I must let him have a copy of that photograph you took.'

'Is it that important?'

Monsieur Pamplemousse shrugged as he picked up the phone. 'Who knows? Two things bother me. One is I don't know the answer to your question. Secondly, someone in the organisation is either a dab hand at second-guessing, or they have a very thorough knowledge of the inner workings of *Le Guide*, including matters that wouldn't or *shouldn't* normally concern them. Also, I wish I knew what it is that Pommes Frites knows and I don't.'

He broke off the moment he was put through.

'Jacques!'

'*Oui. C'est moi...*'

'*Oui*. I am in need of a bit of help ... it won't take long...'

Putting two and two together and making rather more than four, Doucette wandered off for the time being. Aristide's last remark had set her thinking, and as she had foreseen, she had plenty of time on her hands to develop an idea that had entered her mind.

'I thought you implied women hogged the telephone more than men,' she said, when he terminated the call at long last.

'That was different,' said Monsieur Pamplemousse. 'We had important matters to discuss.'

'Ah!' said Doucette. 'Of course. I was for-getting. Women don't, of course. *Vive la dif-férence!*

'In the meantime, I haven't exactly been idle. I have been wondering about Pommes Frites' strange behaviour with the girl's tele-phone. You know that mobile you gave me for my birthday...'

Monsieur Pamplemousse could have said that the reason for his gift had simply been that whenever his mobile was on charge and he wanted to make an important call their main telephone line always seemed to be in use, but he chose the easy way out and simply said 'yes'.

'Well,' said Doucette. 'I have had an idea. I didn't realise I can switch it to what they call vibratory ringing.'

'It had all the optional extras,' said Mon-sieur Pamplemousse. 'I made sure of that.'

'You are very kind, Aristide,' said Dou-cette. 'Well, I had no idea it was possible and I have never had need of the facility until now. I was thinking about Pommes Frites and according to the book of instructions it is specifically aimed at users of importance who wish to avoid disturbing others when they are attending board meetings and need to be contacted urgently, but discreetly...'

200

'I don't see what that has to do with Pommes Frites anyway,' said Monsieur Pamplemousse. 'He wouldn't know a board meeting if he saw one, and he would be bored stiff.'

Doucette reached into her handbag. 'No, but it might be interesting to see how he reacts when this one goes off. Why don't we give it a try and see what happens? You can give me a ring on our main phone while it's free, Aristide. It won't take a moment.'

Monsieur Pamplemousse picked up the phone and prepared to dial. 'What's your number?'

Doucette reached into her handbag again. 'I have it somewhere.'

It took a little while before she found it, but when Monsieur Pamplemousse eventually dialled the right number, albeit through slightly gritted teeth, he could hardly complain. The result was electrifying.

Not much happened on the middle slopes of Montmartre during the winter months so outwardly there was nothing to suggest that Pommes Frites was on the *qui vive*. However, the moment Doucette's mobile began to vibrate his ears shot up, and from a standing start near the window of their apartment, where he had been taking his ease hopefully watching out for what little there was in the

201

way of passing interest in the world outside, to his arrival at her mobile would undoubtedly have broken all records, had there been any in the international edition of the *Guinness Book of Records* to break.

It was an emotional moment as he pivoted on the spot and without a second's hesitation set off down the passage of the Pamplemousses' apartment with the phone in his mouth and scarcely more than a fleeting parting glance.

A keen student of history might have detected an air of finality from the look on his face, akin to that which must have been on the faces of some of those taking part in the Charge of the Light Brigade at Balaclava in 1854, or for that matter, Colonel Custer's last stand against the Sioux Indians at Little Bighorn, Montana, in 1876.

The signal was clear. It said quite simply: 'This is it, lads. Make the most of it. You may never see the like again.'

However, Doucette and Aristide were too taken aback by the speed at which everything had taken place to have registered any such fancy nuances.

'At least we shall be spared the usual ending,' said Monsieur Pamplemousse.

Doucette was about to voice her agreement

when they heard a loud splash.

'Did you leave the *cabinet* door open again, Aristide?' she said accusingly.

'It is, to all intents and purposes, a communal toilet,' said Monsieur Pamplemousse. 'Pommes Frites is my dog, and he lives here.'

'I don't think that gives him the right to use it as a depository for other people's telephones,' said Doucette.

'At least it won't disappear for good,' said Monsieur Pamplemousse.

'Don't you be so sure,' said Doucette. 'You are always saying he watches points. I wouldn't be surprised if he discovered how to flush it given the mood he's in. Besides, it is my birthday present.'

'And it was your idea in the first place,' said Monsieur Pamplemousse. 'You were only too keen to try it out.'

'I didn't expect it to go straight down the pan,' said Doucette. 'But you are absolutely right, Aristide – as ever. You win on points.'

'You won't believe this,' she said on her return, holding the mobile aloft. 'It's still working.'

'I told you I paid extra for the deluxe model,' said Monsieur Pamplemousse. 'The man promised me it was waterproof.'

'What it is to have second sight,' said Doucette. 'But hadn't you better ring off in case you are blocking the line to incoming calls?'

Doing as he was bidden, Monsieur Pamplemousse was rewarded with an instant outside call.

'At last!' said Jacques. 'I thought you were never going to answer. Problems?'

'Don't even ask,' said Monsieur Pamplemousse.

'Just thought you might like to know,' said Jacques. 'I did as you suggested. I had one of my men put your staff list through the computer and Immigration have a query regarding one of your employees. They wouldn't say who because of some regulation or other, but it seems someone has two passports. French plus another and there is a discrepancy of some kind.'

'And the other one?' said Monsieur Pamplemousse

'The UK.'

'How come? Any ideas?'

'Search me,' said Jacques. 'You know as much about these things as I do. Apparently the Immigration people were pretty tight-lipped about it. You know what they're like. But there are ways and means of having more than one passport.'

'Legally?' said Monsieur Pamplemousse.

'Birth ... adoption ... marriage. Although that's more tricky nowadays, particularly when it comes to the UK. The days of a registry office marriage followed by a quickie divorce three days later no longer wash...'

'Forgery?'

'That's a dangerous route, given the latest scanners they have, and getting more so all the time. It's no longer worth the risk.

'I'll get someone to work on it if you like, but if I were you I'd put in a call to your English friend ... the shadowy one who comes and goes. Monsieur...'

'Pickering?'

'That's the one. Used to be in British intelligence. A nice guy, even if he does play his cards close to his chest, at times. A bit like our Customs and Excise, but kosher with it.

'Anyway, my problem is I've been pulled off doing any moonlighting for the time being. So I thought I'd better call you while I have the chance. Funny thing. I'm back to where we came in ... practically the same spot as last time...' He lowered his voice and Monsieur Pamplemousse felt his blood run cold, all thought of what had gone before momentarily wiped from his mind at Jacques' next words.

He cupped both hands over the mouth-piece to shield them from Doucette.

'What's the matter, Aristide?' asked Doucette when he eventually hung up.

'Someone has found a hat floating in the canal St Martin,' said Monsieur Pamplemousse.

'Is that all?'

'It happens,' said Monsieur Pamplemousse. 'And they are following it up. They are searching the canal just in case it means the worst.'

For Doucette's peace of mind he didn't add the hat was red and had clearly belonged to a female. As soon as he mentioned their visitor to Jacques he asked if Doucette would mind having a quick look at it. In his words: 'It's probably a million-to-one chance, but you have to start somewhere...'

CHAPTER NINE

'Eureka!'

Monsieur Pamplemousse nearly fell out of bed with excitement, and for a second or two was unsure as to whether his sudden awakening from a deep slumber had been the result of a particularly vivid dream, or what he'd come to recognise as the early morning departure of a giant Airbus 380 plane taking off from Charles de Gaulle airport and heading over northern Paris.

It didn't matter which of them was the culprit, although if pressed he would have opted for the former, because it would mean that his subconscious had come to the rescue yet again.

During his time with the Sûreté some of his most spectacular cases had been solved by allowing his subconscious to do the spadework for him while he was asleep, and it had rarely let him down.

Not that the current problem had anything to do with a major crime as yet, touch wood, but it had been exercising his mind over the past few days, so he added a *'Sapristi!'* at the top of his voice for good measure.

Conscious of a stirring by his side, he took a firm grip of himself.

'Are you all right, Aristide?' asked Doucette. 'I thought I heard you call out.'

'I think I may have solved it,' he replied. 'I can see it all now. I couldn't at the time ... that was part of the problem. What I took to be an imitation red vein must have been a very fine insulated wire.'

'You are talking a lot of *charabia*, Aristide,' said Doucette sleepily. 'Why don't you come back to bed?'

Monsieur Pamplemousse reached for the bedside light.

'It's as clear as the nose on your face, Couscous,' he said. 'Clearer, in fact.'

'Leave my nose out of it,' said Doucette. 'It isn't five o'clock yet and it probably needs powdering.'

'Point one.' Monsieur Pamplemousse consulted his mental notebook. 'Pommes Frites has been behaving strangely ever since he dropped that fake truffle into the Director's waste bucket, and no wonder.

'Ask yourself, Doucette, what do a truffle and a mobile phone have in common with each other?'

'Nothing as far as I can see,' said Doucette. 'Still less when it's two mobile phones, especially if they're the kind that vibrates when someone makes a call. They vibrate and the truffle doesn't.'

'*Exactement!*' said Monsieur Pamplemousse, triumphantly.

'Don't say you've woken me up just to tell me that!' exclaimed Doucette.

'But, don't you see? What was common to

208

both the mobile phones and the truffle must have been the vibration. Have you ever come across a truffle that vibrated?'

'Not that I have ever noticed,' said Doucette. 'Have you?'

'Dropping the vibrating mobiles into the waste buckets must have been Pommes Frites' way of drawing attention to the fact that this particular fake truffle did,' said Monsieur Pamplemousse. 'Most likely it wasn't strong enough to register with the average human being, but it was sufficient for a dog to wonder what was going on when he had it in his mouth. Since when he must have been racking his brains wondering how on earth he could communicate that simple fact to us all, and to me in particular. Trust him to find a way in the end, even if it did mean having several goes and leaving a trail of unhappy people as a result.

'We live in an age of miniaturisation, and my guess would be that it could have been some kind of state-of-the-art micro recording mechanism; most likely voice operated in order to conserve energy when it wasn't required...'

Doucette sat up in bed, suddenly all attention. 'You mean batteries! What a mercy he didn't swallow the whole thing in his excitement. Think of all that acid entering his system.'

But Monsieur Pamplemousse's mind was racing ahead. He was thinking about where the truffle had been all this time, and there was no getting away from the fact that it must have been in the Director's office when Monsieur Leclercq and Véronique were going through the final review of the entries to next year's guide.

Somebody, somewhere, must have a complete copy of the whole conversation.

'Merde!' There was no other word for it and despite the hour, once again he couldn't avoid expressing his feelings out loud.

Several loud thumps came from the apartment directly overhead.

Doucette buried her head under the duvet and Pommes Frites came running.

Although he was only too conscious of the fact that the technical ramifications of his brainwave must be beyond Pommes Frites' brain cells to grasp in their entirety, Monsieur Pamplemousse tried to plan his next move while at the same time devoting a sizeable amount of time congratulating his ever-faithful friend and mentor on his prowess at getting the all-important message across in such a stylish manner.

In the old days it would have merited a star on his annual report.

He glanced at the bedside clock. It would be another four hours or so before the office opened, and if the truth be known he was beginning to feel the weight of his responsibility as the temporary Head of Security. Monsieur Leclercq would be expecting to see some return for his gesture of faith, and rightly so.

High on the agenda had to be locating the truffle in order to establish whether or not his theory was correct. If it were, then having served its purpose the works inside it would most likely have been removed, or at the very least, the part containing the vital information, in whatever form it took, would have been recovered. Either way it would be one step nearer finding who was behind it all.

Failing that, the obvious course would be to delay publication for an unspecified length of time. The Director would need a lot of persuading to do that. Such a thing had never happened before.

However, a decision on any kind of move would have to wait until later in the morning.

In the meantime going back to bed would be a waste of time. He was too wide awake for that. That said, doing nothing wasn't an option either. Ergo, somehow or other he had to find a worthwhile means of occupying his time while he thought the matter through.

Tidying up a few loose ends perhaps? There was Doucette's worry about the regular appearances of the man with the dog for a start. It would be good to know exactly where he came from. It had to be somewhere nearby, although he didn't sound like a local inhabitant. Given the time of year, he was unlikely to be a holidaymaker.

On the other hand it was equally unlikely that his presence had anything to do with *Le Guide*.

Setting someone on his trail wasn't on the cards now Jacques was tied up, and he didn't have the time to do it himself. Given that man and dog seemed inseparable, perhaps the easy way out would be to put a tag on the dog.

Gathering up his clothing where he had left it before retiring for the night, and having signalled Pommes Frites to follow on behind as quietly as possible, he turned out the light and led the way into the living room.

While he was getting dressed he pondered what Mr Pickering would have to say when he heard the news, or for that matter what he would have to say to Mr Pickering.

There was one matter in the back of his mind which had been bothering him more and more as time went by, but it was an instinctive feeling rather than something concrete he could put into words.

Making for his den, and going back on some of his earlier remarks about emails, he first of all sent a message to Mr Pickering warning him that he needed help; then he searched through the top drawer of his desk until he found a small envelope.

Inside it was a relatively tiny item which was an essential part of one of the many small gifts presented to him when he and Pommes Frites both took early retirement from the Sûreté. Paradoxically it had been given to him by a well-wisher in case the latter had ever shown signs of wanting to go his own way. Perish the thought!

Slipping the envelope into a jacket pocket for the time being, he headed for the kitchen, and having first made sure the door was firmly closed behind them, located the biscuit tin and emptied most of the contents into a bowl, before turning his attention to a food processor.

Pommes Frites licked his lips, clearly hoping it was yet another reward.

'I'm afraid,' said Monsieur Pamplemousse, 'this isn't for you, *mon ami*. You will have to wait until it's your turn.'

He wondered what the Director would have to say if he could see him now.

Underneath his often disarmingly bluff exterior there dwelt a shrewd businessman. *Le Guide* was a large organisation, unique in employing an army of specialists in many different levels. A self-sufficient world in itself, it was comparable to an ocean liner, and in that respect Monsieur Leclercq could lay claim to running a 'tight ship'.

Not simply a 'tight ship', but a happy one, and in Monsieur Pamplemousse's experience that was something which wasn't so much to do with the boss's physical presence, but something more mysterious which began at the top and worked its way down through the company, permeating everything and everybody as it went in what was really a process of osmosis.

It was a rare gift; one that was infinitely worth protecting and it strengthened his own desire to make sure it remained intact while he had anything to do with it.

Having ground the biscuits to a fine sandy consistency, he mixed in an equal quantity of plain flour. Then he opened a jar marked SUCRE and added four or five tablespoonfuls of its yellowish, but equally powdery contents.

Following that with a generous slab of butter and some milk from a bottle, he gave the whole another whirl with the mixer until it began showing signs of forming a dough. At which point he hastily switched off the Magimix and transferred the contents onto a breadboard.

It had been guesswork so far, and mercifully Doucette seemed to have slept through it all, but feeling more than pleased with his handiwork, he turned the oven on and relaxed for a moment or two while he gave Pommes Frites the remains of the biscuits.

Another thing about Monsieur Leclercq. He wasn't simply a figurehead who had never got his hands dirty, as one might suppose listening to him at times. He had started out as a junior inspector and a very able and conscientious one at that by all accounts. The founder of *Le Guide*, Monsieur Hippolyte Duval, would never have handed over the reins when he retired had it been otherwise, and his faith had not been misplaced.

It was all before his own time, of course, but once in the saddle Monsieur Leclercq had also revealed an uncanny aptitude when it came to engaging new staff. It was one of the main reasons why under his guidance *Le Guide* had gone from strength to strength over the years.

Which made it all the more surprising that he had employed Barnaud almost on sight as it were. *And* entrusted him with a highly responsible job into the bargain. Perhaps his eagerness to get going with the new app had clouded his judgement and he was anxious to leave no stone unturned.

The press office had already gone to town on the subject of the apps. Teasers had been appearing in the press. There was no going back.

Barnaud was certainly a smooth talker, but over and above that, it struck Monsieur Pamplemousse that there was something about him which didn't ring true.

He also couldn't rid himself of the feeling that he had seen him before somewhere.

During his time with the Sûreté he had acquired a built-in extrasensory perception about people, and although he had nothing concrete to go on, he wondered if perhaps for once the Director had made a mistake.

He wasn't alone when he said that. Véronique echoed his feelings. Apparently something untoward had taken place when she had tried to take a photograph of Bar-

naud soon after he arrived. Monsieur Leclercq liked to keep a pictorial record of
what he called his 'core staff', and Barnaud
flatly refused to cooperate.

Detaching a handful of his mixture he set
about moulding it into the shape of a bone,
dusting it with some flour before laying it
out on a sheet of foil to rest. Then, in Doucette's absence, he took a chance and set the
oven to 200°C – a figure he had often heard
her mention in conversations with her sister
Agathe, who was always phoning for advice
on culinary matters.

He wondered if perhaps Barnaud was the
person the immigration people had set their
sights on. Although he couldn't really
quantify what was merely a feeling in the
back of his mind, it wouldn't surprise him.

Returning to his handiwork, he held it up
to the light. There was enough dough left
over to make several more exactly like it, but
for what he had in mind one bone would be
quite sufficient. It would either work or it
wouldn't. More would only confuse matters.

Having made a suitable hole in the side he
decided to take the plunge. It would need to
cool down before he inserted the homing
tag he'd taken from his desk drawer, and
certainly before any dog, however hungry,

217

would take it into its head to devour it.

The need for it to be put into position at an appropriate time was crucial. Not too soon for fear of another dog finding it first, but certainly before they were spotted doing it.

He glanced around the kitchen. It was in a mess. Somehow or other he seemed to have used far more utensils than he had intended.

Shortly before 08.00 he went outside in order to find a suitable spot at the side of the road to place the bone where he could keep a watchful eye on it from on high. Settling for a spot near the wall to one side of the square, where a statue of the writer Marcel Aymé's famous creation *The Man Who Could Walk Through Walls* appeared to be doing just that, he set to work. Hopefully, being low on the ground, the dog would spot it long before its master did.

He was only just in time. Even as he bent down to rest the bone in a small pile of leaves, he caught sight of some figures approaching up the hill, so he hurried back inside the apartment block.

Luck was with him. The lift was still where he had left it on the ground floor and he was back on the seventh in double-quick time.

He hurried across to the living-room

window, and sure enough, on the far side of the Place Marcel Aymé a small black dog was busying itself with the bone, while Doucette's *bête noire* stood to one side apparently talking into a handset.

It seemed a satisfactory outcome after all his labours, but before he had time to dwell on it the phone rang.

Mr Pickering was a committed Francophile and enjoyed catching up on news from across La Manche no matter what time of day it was, but it was something of a record even for him.

'I got your call, Aristide,' he said. *'Comment ça va?'*

'I am well enough,' said Monsieur Pamplemousse after the preliminaries had been disposed of, 'but we have a problem with a member of staff. It has to do with their passport, or perhaps I should say, passports. The person concerned has two – one French and the other British, and apparently there is something about them that doesn't tally. The powers that be are dragging their heels about it, but the question is which one is bothering them? I was hoping you could help with the British end. It couldn't have happened at a worse time. We are coming up to publication and you know how twitchy the Director gets about any kind of scandal.'

'Do you know who the person is?'

'It is purely guesswork, but it has to be someone who joined us recently and I do have someone in mind. The trouble is that although he came to us with impeccable references, I don't entirely trust him.'

'In what way exactly?'

'He can be somewhat economical with the truth.' Monsieur Pamplemousse gave a brief rundown of his meeting with Barnaud in the canteen, when he extolled the virtues of Line 14 on the Metro.

'He made it sound as though he used it every day of his life, whereas in retrospect I doubt if he had ever been on it in his life. It was all textbook stuff. Also, alas, he is not a true Frenchman.'

'How so?'

'Little things. *Par exemple*, he doesn't hold his champagne glass by the stem. While he was talking to me he gripped the bowl in his hot little hands as though there was no tomorrow, which was a dead giveaway.'

'*Oh, là là*,' said Mr Pickering, dryly. 'What *is* the world coming to?'

'*And*,' continued Monsieur Pamplemousse, 'when he needed a refill, instead of simply holding up a thumb, indicating a single glass, he used his index finger and then got cross when two glasses arrived, although I have to admit it was to my benefit.'

'Say no more,' said Mr Pickering. 'He sounds as if he is what we call a thoroughly bad egg.'

'A bad egg?' repeated Monsieur Pample-mousse. *'Je ne comprends pas.'*

'Bad eggs are problem people,' said Mr Pickering. 'And it's getting worse all the time. No doubt you French have a word for them.'

'Les sales?' ventured Monsieur Pample-mousse.

'How splendid,' said Mr Pickering. 'I knew you wouldn't let me down, Aristide. You people have a phrase for most things. In the UK the use of the word "egg" to describe a bad person has been around since Shakes-peare's time. When he was writing *Macbeth*, he had some murderers say to Macduff's son: "What, you egg! Young fry of treachery!" while they despatched him.

'Only in recent times have there been good eggs and I fear they are in danger of becom-ing extinct. During the last war when food was rationed and real eggs were precious, a bad one could be taken back to the supplier in a bowl and replaced with a good one. I sometimes wish that same procedure could be applied to present-day felons.

'Anyway, enough of that. I gather you have a problem.'

Monsieur Pamplemousse hesitated. Mr Pickering sounded more detached than usual. 'If you prefer it,' he said, 'I can phone back on another day.'

'Forgive me,' said Mr Pickering. 'I was taking advantage of a friendly ear. In the past few months my wife and I have experienced a burglary, and along with it the temporary loss of our front door. So we had to address visitors through the letter box when we told them to use the back door. All very inconvenient.

'To quote Shakespeare again, we have been "suffering the slings and arrows of outrageous fortune" and it's entirely my own fault for taking an eye off the ball. I have been left with egg on my face.'

'My turn to ask for forgiveness,' said Monsieur Pamplemousse. 'But wasn't there someone in one of Monsieur Shakespeare's plays who said: "There is something rotten in the state of Denmark"?'

'*Hamlet*, and it was a character called Marcellus,' said Mr Pickering.

'Well, I am currently suffering in much the same way,' said Monsieur Pamplemousse.

'Only it isn't in Scandinavia, it's right here in Paris, France.'

'I am all ears,' said Mr Pickering. 'It sounds just the thing for a "buck-me-up".'

Monsieur Pamplemousse wondered if he should burden him with his other fears regarding the truffle, but hearing footsteps approaching he decided against it.

'Time for your early morning coffee and biscuits, Aristide!' called Doucette, as she went past.

'I didn't know you were a biscuit man,' said Mr Pickering.

'I'm not,' hissed Monsieur Pamplemousse. 'That's another problem I have, but I think I may have found a solution...'

'Is it urgent?' asked Mr Pickering. 'I mean the business with the passport.'

'Publication day is on Tuesday,' said Monsieur Pamplemousse. 'In three days' time.'

'Is it possible to have a photograph of your suspect?' said Mr Pickering hastily. 'I'll get on to it straight away and ring you back as soon as possible.'

'I will do my best,' said Monsieur Pamplemousse. Knowing Véronique, he doubted if she had let Barnaud off without something in her camera.

'What on earth has been going on, Aristide?' said Doucette, as he made his way into the kitchen. 'Look at it! I have never seen such a mess.'

'Don't worry, Couscous,' said Monsieur Pamplemousse. 'I was about to clear it all up.'

Doucette reached for her apron. 'I'd rather do it myself, thank you very much,' she said.

'I was making a bone for that dog you keep telling me about,' said Monsieur Pamplemousse. 'It was for your benefit. I thought that since he and his master seem inseparable I could make use of my tracking device and it will lead me to where they both live. It's been lying idle for far too long.

'I would have followed it up straight away, but I had an important phone call from Mr Pickering. Anyway, all is not lost. If the dog has eaten all the bone it must have swallowed the homing tag, so I can still pick up the signal the next time it passes.'

Doucette began her tidying up. 'If you used all these things to make a dog's bone, I would hate to have you around when you cook a three-course dinner.'

She picked up the tin marked SUCRE.

'What were you doing with my mother's old tin?'

'I thought the dog might have a sweet

tooth,' said Monsieur Pamplemousse.

'Sweet?' Doucette gave a hollow laugh.

'Is that a problem?' asked Monsieur Pamplemousse.

'Only the fact that it isn't sugar.'

'What is it then?'

'It is a very strong laxative,' said Doucette.

Monsieur Pamplemousse stared at her. 'So why is it marked SUCRE?'

'Because my mother had nowhere else to put it,' said Doucette. 'She would have known what was in the tin and to her way of thinking that would have been sufficient. I hadn't the heart to throw it away when she died. It reminds me of her funny little ways.'

'But...' Monsieur Pamplemousse was suddenly at a loss for words.

'How long is it since we got married, Aristide?' said Doucette. 'She died two years before that.'

Monsieur Pamplemousse didn't answer for fear of getting it wrong.

'She used it on me when I was small,' said Doucette, nostalgically. 'One teaspoonful before I went to school on a Monday went a very long way. It saw me safely through the week.'

'How about four or five tablespoonfuls?' said Monsieur Pamplemousse, in dismay.

'You haven't...' said Doucette.

'I thought it was funny-looking sugar,' he admitted.

'Thank goodness you don't do the cooking,' said Doucette. 'I would say if it still does its stuff the explosion will give us a good idea of where they live. It will be in all the journals. On the other hand, since it must be well past its sell-by date that may never happen. If you want my opinion, Aristide, I suggest for the next few days it will be a case of watch this space.'

CHAPTER TEN

It was the following day before Mr Pickering phoned again.

'Sorry to call you so early on a Sunday morning,' he said, 'but needs must.'

'It's that time of the year,' said Monsieur Pamplemousse. 'There are no weekends before publication day.'

'Quite right, too,' said Mr Pickering. 'People tend to take their utilities for granted, so why should *Le Guide* be an exception. Tell me, do you French use the word *scam?*'

'Scam?' repeated Monsieur Pamplemousse. 'I don't even know what it stands
for.'

'The *Oxford English Dictionary* has it down
as meaning "a trick or swindle, a fraud",'
said Mr Pickering.

'I think we have our share of all three,' said
Monsieur Pamplemousse. 'Even on a Sunday. But we don't make use of that word.'

'Then you should,' said Mr Pickering. 'In
England it is common currency.'

'In France,' said Monsieur Pamplemousse,
'these things take time. It has to go before a
panel of forty *académiciens* known as the
Immortels to receive their approval before it
can enter the dictionary. They publish a list of
acceptable words every three months.'

'Three months!' echoed Mr Pickering.
'I'm talking about the next day or two.'

Monsieur Pamplemousse gave a shrug.
'*C'est normal.* I'm not sure what they will
think about a word like "scam". It doesn't
sound very nice.'

'It isn't very nice,' said Mr Pickering. 'And
the reason why I'm phoning so early is
because I have a feeling one might be heading your way right now and there is no time
to lose if you are to nip it in the bud.'

'Did you get the photograph of Barnaud?'

asked Monsieur Pamplemousse.

'I did indeed, thank you very much,' said Mr Pickering. 'And therein lies the rub. In the English passport his name is down as Barnard, which was his mother's maiden name.

'He was born into a mixed family – a French father and an English mother, and at some point in his early life there was a major break-up when his father, Monsieur Dupois, was sent to prison. His mother, presumably unable to cope on her own, sent her son to England to stay with a relative while he completed his schooling. It was then that he adopted her old surname, probably to avoid the disgrace hanging over him. It may even have been her idea.'

'How about the change to Barnaud on his French passport?' asked Monsieur Pamplemousse.

'That must have crept in some years later when he completed his education at a technical college in Grenoble,' said Mr Pickering. 'Such things were much easier to bring about in those days.

'Anyway, to cut a long story short, at Grenoble he seems to have taken to the world of computers like a fish to water. So much so, on his return to the UK, he was in big demand.

'Unfortunately he must have inherited some of his father's ways, because he seems to have blotted his copybook while he was working for a bank. Until that date he had been getting good reports. Then he suddenly left under a cloud.'

'Have you any idea what the reason was?'

'Who knows?' said Mr Pickering. 'Banks can be very unforthcoming when they choose. They dislike any publicity that reflects on their probity. At one time anyone kicking over the traces or engaged in minor fraud...'

'Such as?' broke in Monsieur Pamplemousse.

'Getting old ladies to press harder with their ballpoint pens on trumped-up documents, so that their signature could be accurately forged with a view to making tiny withdrawals from their account. If the amount was very small it usually escaped notice, but over a period of time it could mount up – and it was tax free!

'If they were caught they were quietly shown the door, never to be seen again.

'Times change, and money being the root of all evil so did the size of the scams. When it started to involve thousands of pounds, or in some cases millions, it no longer came under the heading of "inappropriate behaviour" and the police were called in. Result? The culprits hit the headlines and end up doing time.

'Barnaud escaped the ignominy of the first. He wasn't doing counter work. Instead, he was behind the scenes glued to a computer, which probably gave him much more scope for nefarious practices before he was made redundant. As I say, we shall never know.

'All we do know is that being "made redundant" was probably a euphemism for something shady because he wasn't given a reference. As a consequence he dropped out of the computer world altogether for a while and tried his luck in other fields.

'He didn't stick at anything for very long. For a while he even found work as an up-market carpet layer; which is when he first came to the notice of the police.' Mr Pickering paused for breath. 'Stop me if I am boring you.'

'Not at all,' said Monsieur Pamplemousse. 'I am all ears. I hear bells ringing in all directions.'

'His work took him to some wealthy homes,' continued Mr Pickering. 'Homes which in many instances housed valuable works of art. Works of art that from time to time caused burglars to pay a visit not long after the carpet layers had departed...

'Surprise!... Surprise! The upshot of that was the police, as is their wont, began putting two and two together and started asking questions.

'Incidentally, those sunglasses Barnaud wears ... they may look trendy, but the frames contain a high-definition camcorder able to record up to ninety minutes of video, both sound and vision.'

'What will they think of next?' said Monsieur Pamplemousse. 'That answers another question.'

'I had a pair myself once,' said Mr Pickering. 'Very enlightening they were too, until Mrs Pickering sat on them.'

'Not while you were wearing them I trust,' said Monsieur Pamplemousse.

'Perish the thought,' said Mr Pickering. He paused. 'By now you may well be wondering what all this is leading up to.'

'I must admit,' said Monsieur Pamplemousse, 'I hold no great brief for Barnaud, quite the reverse in fact, but he does seem to have found his niche at last. What bothers me is that before being taken on it was his suggestion that Monsieur Leclercq should first of all check his credentials thoroughly, and to that end he even provided the telephone number of a professor at his old college. It was a direct line, so the Director got through straight away and after suffering some difficulty in establishing his own credentials, he received a glowing report on Barnaud's achievements.'

'And no doubt,' broke in Mr Pickering, 'having given him a glowing report, the professor insisted on passing him on to someone higher up. The dean, perhaps?'

Monsieur Pamplemousse fell silent.

'I could write the script, Aristide,' said Mr Pickering bluntly.

'I don't doubt for one moment that had Monsieur Leclercq tried to ring back, perhaps to thank them for all the trouble they had gone to, he would have found the number didn't exist. The people involved were most likely all in the same room. Barnard and his associates are past masters at the art of make-believe and they carry others along with them.

'The big scam currently taking place over here is credit-card theft over the phone. Usually it takes place in the evening when the banks are closed and it takes the form of a cold call from someone purporting to be an employee of a credit-card security firm who tells the victim their bank account has been compromised.

'First of all he asks if they used their card recently to withdraw cash from a machine, quoting an unusually large sum of money from a bank in an out-of-the-way area at an unlikely time of night.

'Naturally the victim denies having done any such thing. At the same time their heart most likely misses a beat which is a plus point for the caller.

'The voice then says that in order to establish their caller's credentials the victim should hang up and call an official number, for example the one on the back of their credit card. All very reassuring at a time when reassurance is most needed.

'However, unknown to the victim, the line has been kept open and their call goes straight back to the original caller who pretends he is a member of the bank staff, much as happened with your Director when he thought he was talking to the professor at a technical college.

'At which point the voice at the other end, having expressed his sympathy, says they must move swiftly to put a stop on the victim's card, along with any others they may possess and, since he has direct lines to the various banks, given the relevant details, he will gladly save valuable time by doing it for them there and then. He will, of course, need to check the PIN number to make sure there are no mistakes.

'Leaving a colleague to offer a few more words of sympathy he returns after a suitable gap with the news that all the cards named have had a stop put on them, so they might just as well be thrown in the dustbin.

'Except – as he is about to say goodnight, a sudden thought strikes him. It is just possible they might be able to retrieve some valuable information off the black band on the back of the cards. It would be very helpful if they could be put into an envelope for safekeeping. Meanwhile he will arrange for a courier to pick them up.

'By the time the victims wake up the next morning copies will have been made and put to use in as many cashpoints as possible.'

'And people fall for that kind of thing?' said Monsieur Pamplemousse.

'That's easily said,' replied Mr Pickering. 'But don't forget that in a different context your Director was taken in by a phone call.

'In the cold light of day a lot of the people

who have been victims of similar scams must wonder how on earth it happened, but it is carried out with such panache and air of authority it's all too easy to go along with it. The world is their oyster.

'Scams aren't confined to the hoi polloi. Take the man who set up a company called Global Technical Ltd, and made millions selling little black boxes with an aerial sticking out the side. Labelled GT200, he claimed it was a bomb-disposal device, and people who should have known better queued up in countries all over the world to buy it.

'All very rich considering he must have got the idea from a Mr McCormick who based his earlier model on a novelty lost-golf-ball finder, and is now serving ten years in gaol. These people never give up.

'Listen, Aristide, if you are waiting to see a specialist in a hospital and someone wearing a nurse's uniform pops their head round the door saying "would you please take off all your clothes and put them in this bag, then stand on the scales until you are called", what do you do?'

'Until a moment or so ago I would have stripped off,' said Monsieur Pamplemousse. 'Now. I'm not so sure.'

'Very wise,' said Mr Pickering. 'There is

always the possibility you might never see your clothes again and half an hour later you would be feeling an idiot, shivering, and calling for help.

'Anyway, getting back to Barnard, to use his English name, it seems that having been linked with the credit-card scam, he disappeared off the radar screen some weeks ago and, always presuming my information that Barnard and Barnaud are one and the same person is correct, he and his associates are now at large somewhere in France.

'He must have another trick up his sleeve, and we all know where that might be, even if we don't know what or when.'

Monsieur Pamplemousse thanked him. The leap from fashioning dog bones to the rather more sophisticated world of credit-card scams wasn't exactly of quantum proportions, but it did take a lot of assimilating in one go.

'Is that nice secretary of Monsieur Leclercq's still with you?' asked Mr Pickering. 'The one who always puts me in mind of Miss Moneypenny in a James Bond film?'

'Véronique? I'm not sure if she will thank you, but she is an essential part of the furniture and fittings,' said Monsieur Pamplemousse. He looked at his watch. 'I doubt if she is in just yet. In the meantime I'm working from home.' He went on to explain about his digression with the dog biscuit.

'I do like a dog that combines business with pleasure,' said Mr Pickering. 'I suggest when she does arrive you get her to phone you immediately if anyone pays an unexpected visit to the Director without prior appointment. I have a feeling if anything is going to happen, it will happen soon. Once these people have set their sights on something there is no stopping them. Speed is of the essence, and whatever it is they have in mind there will be no going back.'

'In the meantime I shall keep my credit cards under wraps,' said Monsieur Pamplemousse.

'I hope they will be the least of your worries,' said Mr Pickering, staving off the wave of thanks that came over the line for his prompt response.

'I would love to be with you, Aristide,' was his gloomy response, 'but I doubt if I shall make it in time.'

As it happened, Véronique arrived much earlier than usual and she phoned him to report straight away. He wondered if he should warn her about his conversation with Mr Pickering and decided not to for the time being. He knew he could trust her, and too many details might be an unwanted distraction.

He also knew from a conversation he'd had with her when he enquired if she had managed to take a photograph of Barnaud that the answer was 'Yes', and for reasons unstated she wished she hadn't and she was glad to get rid of it.

There was also the barest of possibilities that Pickering was mistaken in his prognosis. He put her slightly nervous tone down to pre-publication jitters, and with the unveiling of the new app scheduled for the morrow who wouldn't be tense?

'Is Barnaud in yet?' he asked. He very nearly asked if Barnard was in!

'He wasn't answering his phone yesterday,' said Véronique. 'And there is a *PASSAGE INTERDIT* notice hanging outside the door of his room on the third floor. Madame Grante's getting quite huffy about it. She's taken against him.'

She didn't add 'that makes two of us'. Instead, she broke into a passing good imitation of *Le Guide's* Head of Accounts giving vent to her displeasure.

'Nobody cares two hoots about disturbing *me,* nor ever has!'

'I should save it for next year's summer party,' said Monsieur Pamplemousse.

'I don't mind living dangerously,' said Véronique. 'But only up to a point. There is a limit to everything. There's nothing like the real thing. Beware of imitations, I say!'

'Beware of imitations!' Quite literally, as he replaced the receiver those few words struck Monsieur Pamplemousse like a thunderbolt from out of the blue.

He could have kicked himself. Beware of imitations! The likeness had been there all the time, staring him in the face. No wonder Madame Grante had taken against Barnaud. On the other side of the coin he was surprised the Director hadn't noticed it, but then he wasn't the most observant of people.

It was no wonder their latest recruit had never been without his dark glasses. Pickering may have been right about them from one point of view. They probably did serve a useful purpose from time to time. But seen from another angle the main purpose of wearing them must have been to hide behind. The sheer gall of it! Talk about entering the lion's den with gay abandon!

A quick call back to Mr Pickering confirmed his worst fears.

The family row he had spoken of had taken

place in Belfort, in the Franche-Comté, involving a young chef who, having inherited a two-Stock Pot restaurant from his father, had been caught attempting to pass off a chicken from the local supermarket as a *poularde de Bresse*.

'In France, there being no greater crime in the catering world than the heinous offence of passing-off, the chef was immediately ostracised both by the general public and his fellow practitioners all over France, and ultimately he was sent to prison.

'I won't go into the repercussions. Suffice to say they were not pleasant. Naked revenge never is.'

'You know who was responsible for catching him at it?' said Monsieur Pamplemousse.

Mr Pickering had to confess he didn't.

'Monsieur Leclercq! It was his first tour of duty, and it was largely the way he handled the case and dug his heels in until the bitter end, despite nearly being knifed, that caused the founder of *Le Guide* to earmark him for bigger things.'

'You think perhaps this a chance to kill two birds with one stone on behalf of his father?' suggested Mr Pickering.

'I have already told Doucette it feels like a case of history repeating itself,' said Monsieur Pamplemousse. 'Now I am sure of it.'

'It is very apt to do so,' said Mr Pickering. 'There is nothing unusual in that. As the Irish author James Joyce once said: "History is a nightmare from which I am trying to awake."'

'*Merci beaucoup*,' said Monsieur Pamplemousse.

'He did have a way with words,' said Mr Pickering, by way of comfort.

And so began what seemed at the time the longest day of Monsieur Pamplemousse's career. The weather didn't help. The sky was grey and the hills surrounding Paris were shrouded in mist. The forecast on the radio didn't offer much in the way of hope for an early improvement.

The one bright spot was when Jacques phoned to say he was now available if required: 'Anything – it doesn't matter what. Masonics, fêtes ... rescuing maidens from burning buildings a speciality...'

But even Jacques seemed to be affected by the elements, unusually *subfusc* was his way of putting it, and it was catching – everyone else in his section was the same. So the conversation was unusually short and sweet. Having jokingly asked for the offer in writing, Monsieur Pamplemousse returned to his window gazing.

On a sunny spring day it was possible to see beyond the southern stretch of the Paris Périphérique and the stadium at the Porte de Châtillon, but today he could barely make out the top of the Eiffel Tower half the distance away.

To say it matched his mood would have been putting it mildly. Even Pommes Frites closed his eyes in order to shut himself off from the world outside. One brief glance was sufficient.

Doucette's analogy with a spider's web was nearer the truth than he'd realised,' except the web had not attached itself to *Le Guide* by chance, but with malice afore-thought. In all probability Barnaud had been involved with the original scam in the restaurant. It would figure. He wouldn't put it past him. Although he had to admire his audacity in virtually manufacturing a job with *Le Guide*, the reality was a case of a little knowledge being a dangerous thing. He was certainly a quick learner, but he was also skating on very thin ice.

Introducing a girl to play the part of Caterina, who could deliver and pick up the truffle when required and with no questions asked was pushing it a bit; although Monsieur

Leclercq's wife being away and nobody else as far he could make out knowing what she looked like would have seemed a stroke of luck.

He must have hired a budding thespian looking for acting experience, who in the end got more than she had bargained for and went off in a panic.

The news that the Director had arranged for someone who really did know Caterina to meet the train must have been a nasty moment, especially when the stand-in reported back to say Monsieur Leclercq insisted she was to stay with the Pamplemousses. It must have felt as though his whole world was collapsing about his ears.

It was a wonder he hadn't thrown the sponge in at that point.

For all he knew there were others in the plot, but that was enough to occupy his thoughts for the time being.

Véronique's call came through a minute or so after 16.00. 'He's been and gone,' she said. 'He said he was a courier, but he didn't look like one to me. Couriers don't usually come dressed in a long black overcoat.

'He had a dog with him, too. A little black one with a beard...'

'And a tail that sticks straight up in the

air?' broke in Monsieur Pamplemousse, wondering what Doucette would say when she heard. 'I told you so!' in all probability.

'Anything but, if you ask me,' said Véronique. 'Definitely at half mast. It was looking very sorry for itself.

'Even at that, he had nothing on the Director. He looked shattered after they left. I think it has to do with a cheque... God knows how much it's for...'

'Put me through,' said Monsieur Pamplemousse.

'He's not taking any calls, I'm afraid,' said Véronique.

'Tell him it's an emergency.'

'Not from anyone,' said Véronique. 'And when Monsieur Leclercq says "no one" he means "no one", not even you, Aristide. It's as much as my job is worth.'

'Well,' said Monsieur Pamplemousse. 'Here's what I suggest you do. You walk into his office and you tell him I don't care how much the cheque is for, or whom it is for, he must put a stop on it straight away. Furthermore, if he doesn't, he will have lost his temporary Head of Security. End of conversation.'

'May I tell you something?' said Véronique. 'I would much rather you do it for me.'

'I would if I could,' said Monsieur Pamplemousse. 'But we have an emergency on our hands. I need to be elsewhere. There is something else I would like to know first of all. How did they arrive and how did they leave?'

'I don't know how they arrived,' said Véronique. 'Somebody must have let them in the back way. But according to old Rambaud on the gate, when they left they picked up an empty taxi which was heading down from the rank at the Place de Santiago-de-Chile. He thinks the dog was in a bit of a hurry. The way he scrambled into the back you would have thought there was no to-morrow. The man seemed to be having a bit of an argument with the driver.'

Monsieur Pamplemousse slammed the receiver back into its cradle and felt in his jacket pocket. There was no time to be lost.

Having made sure the locator was still there, and following the briefest of farewells to Doucette, he was out of the building in less than three minutes. As he ran past Ciné 13 on the opposite corner, he paused to switch on the sensor and then headed off down the avenue Junot as fast as he could go with Pommes Frites hot on his heels.

For the first fifty metres or so there wasn't

the slightest reaction from the sensor and he was about to give hope when, as they reached the long bend to the right and drew near the Villa Léandre he came to a sudden halt on hearing a stream of pips.

In all the time he had lived in the area he had never really taken in the Villa Léandre. Short and sweet, it was like a picture-post-card with its rows of flower-draped porches and tiny front gardens. In the summer it must be a blaze of colour, but the first thing that caught his eye was the pavement to their right.

Clearly, it was where the taxi had stopped in order to disgorge its passengers.

And not a moment too soon by the look of it.

He could picture the argument that must have gone on. Probably in any other avenue or street in Paris it would have brought the inhabitants running out of their homes, but the Villa Léandre looked serenely unruffled; as quiet as the cloisters in a nunnery.

Signalling Pommes Frites to keep a watch-ful eye out, he made his way cautiously along the short length of the street; making mental notes as he went according to the strength of the signal given out by the sensor. As soon as it reached its peak outside one of the houses near the far end, he turned and beat a hasty retreat to the avenue Junot for fear of being spotted.

As soon as they were back home he dialled Jacques' emergency number and after as succinct a summing-up as possible issued his directions.

'Call me when you get near the Cimetière St Vincent and I will direct you from then on,' he said.

There was an answering *'D'accord'* from Jacques and the line went dead.

It seemed an age, but in fact it was only a matter of minutes before he heard the sound of a siren in the distance, and shortly afterwards Jacques called back.

'Turn off the rue Caulaincourt at the Place Constantin Pecqueur and turn right into the avenue Junot,' said Monsieur Pample-mousse. 'I suggest no sirens from now on. The road curves round anticlockwise in virtually a half circle. Near the end of the curve you will see several upmarket estate agents on your right. Their windows are full of pictures of properties to let. Just past the last one turn into the Villa Léandre. It's very short and on the right near the far end is where I think you will find them. There is a trail of merde de chien on the *trottoir*...

'No, it isn't Pommes Frites'...

'It's the third *dôme de caca* on the right ... you can't miss it.'

His words were lost momentarily as the vehicle skidded to a halt.

'I said you can't miss it,' he repeated.

'Do you want to bet?' said Jacques. 'The super has just trodden in it!'

'Ask him if he could look out for a homing tag when he scrapes it clean,' said Monsieur Pamplemousse. 'It's the only one I've got.'

There was a moment's pause.

'Loosely translated,' said Jacques, 'it's along the lines of "he really shouldn't ask me to do things like that at a time like this when I'm up to my knees in *baiser merde*".

'I'd better phone you back,' he added. 'We're about to ring the front doorbell.'

His words were punctuated by the familiar crash of a battering ram and moments later, after the phone went dead, there came the sound of shots being fired.

'Oh, dear,' said Doucette. 'I hope that little Scottie will be all right.'

'It's probably put him off home-made biscuits for some time to come,' said Monsieur Pamplemousse.

'Ah!' said Doucette. 'Thank you for reminding me, Aristide. That's another thing

I've been meaning to ask you about.'

It was some while before the Villa Léandre regained what was left of its cloistered peace, and what with one thing and another it was dark by the time Monsieur Pamplemousse was able to take Pommes Frites for his evening constitutional.

There had been no sign of Barnaud in the Villa Léandre, and his companion having been whisked off to hospital under an armed guard, by general agreement the unravelling of what everyone had at last come to realise comprised a web of intrigue was put on hold.

Rather than wander aimlessly around the area in front of their apartment block, and wishing to have an aim in view, Monsieur Pamplemousse led the way down the side of the block towards the tiny Place Dalida at the top of some steps leading down from the Butte to the Lamarck-Caulaincourt Métro station.

The square was home to a large bust honouring the renowned singer's life-long multilingual achievements in the world of stage, screen and cabaret, and not for the first time he fell to wondering how such an extraordinarily beautiful, talented and popular performer, winner of innumerable gold discs and judged second only to President de Gaulle in a vote nominating the person who'd had the greatest impact on French society, could not only have left behind a trail of suicidal lovers, but had ended up taking her own life.

Perhaps in the end it was simply a case of cause and effect.

Making his way back home Monsieur Pamplemousse paused for a moment by the Impasse Girardon while he waited for Pommes Frites to catch up with him. In its way the narrow alley had become as chic and sought after as the Villa Léandre and at night the street lamps lent it an air of enchantment...

Aware of a presence joining him, he was about move on when a single shot rang out, and silhouetted in their light, his friend and mentor slid slowly to the ground and lay motionless at his feet.

It was not for nothing that Pommes Frites had been awarded the Pierre Armand Golden Bone Trophy for being best sniffer dog of the year during his time with the Paris Sûreté. Nor, in fact, did the naming of the award do it full justice, for the requirements covered many other talents besides sniffing.

The ability to follow a scent days after a crime had been committed was a given; that was what he and the rest of the team were all about. But being able to open doors by grasping the handle in his mouth and turning it was another accomplishment that went with the job. And like many of his colleagues who were destined to come up against the rougher elements of humanity from time to time, he had undergone not one, but many sessions on the firing range being exposed to the sound of gunfire at close quarters, and like the others on his course he learnt to take such things in his stride, without losing for one moment the quality they had become renowned for, honed to perfection by the Monks of St Hubert in Belgium; that of being basically good-natured. They simply couldn't help themselves. It had been in their genes for over a thousand years.

So when, after a moment or two, sensing something untoward was about to happen, Pommes Frites rose to his feet, Monsieur Pamplemousse wasn't unduly surprised. He had been expecting it. After all, it was what he had been trained to do in an emergency: play possum and watch points.

Barnaud, on the other hand, who had

been creeping up behind him knowing none of these things, was taken completely by surprise.

So when Pommes Frites, smelling fear in the air, wrapped his teeth firmly round his wrist, the article he was holding not only went flying, but in trying to drag his arm free he met up with totally unexpected resistance.

It was a classic case of the immovable object up against the irresistible force, and when at last Barnaud did manage to drag himself free he disappeared into the night leaving a trail of blood in his wake.

And so began a whole new chapter.

Barnaud had actually done his stuff admirably, and apart from a doctored version of his app there was an impeccable original which was duly published on the Tuesday to much acclaim from all the food writers of note, who applauded *Le Guide's* move into the computer age.

Monsieur Pamplemousse never did get his homing tag back, but then he hoped he wouldn't need it again, and he soon forgot about it when a case of his favourite Gosset champagne was delivered, compliments of Monsieur Leclercq.

Shortly afterwards a cardboard box arrived and inside it there was a red hat along with a note apologising for any unnecessary worry finding it in the canal might have caused and thanking them both for their hospitality. It was unsigned.

The Director's wife, when she returned from what she referred to as "a successful outing in Switzerland", couldn't resist telling her uncle the full story, to which he replied: 'Don't you worry your pretty little head about it. I will see what can be arranged. That kind of thing gives the Mafia a bad name.'

Which Monsieur Pamplemousse thought was a satisfactory ending to what could have been a particularly unsatisfactory episode, although he wouldn't fancy being in Barnaud's shoes. He only had to look at the object Barnaud had dropped on that near-fatal night to lose any sympathy he might have had. In fact his blood ran cold. A carpet punch is not a pretty sight.

What pleased him most of all, and Doucette too, was that Véronique took over the management of the masterless Scottie, by now fully recovered from his indisposition.

She named him Mr Magoo, which seemed eminently suitable and most mornings he graced the streets surrounding *Le Guide's* offices before she came in to work. For the rest of the day he was given full run of the balcony on the seventh floor, and Monsieur Leclercq derived much pleasure from seeing the tip of his black tail go past his picture window from time to time during the day.

Unfailingly bolt upright, it was what Mr Pickering would have called a Happy Ending.

The publishers hope that this book has given you enjoyable reading. Large Print Books are especially designed to be as easy to see and hold as possible. If you wish a complete list of our books please ask at your local library or write directly to:

Magna Large Print Books
Magna House, Long Preston,
Skipton, North Yorkshire.
BD23 4ND

This Large Print Book, for people
who cannot read normal print,
is published under the auspices of

THE ULVERSCROFT FOUNDATION

... we hope you have enjoyed this book.
Please think for a moment about those
who have worse eyesight than you ...
and are unable to even read or enjoy
Large Print without great difficulty.

You can help them by sending a
donation, large or small, to:

**The Ulverscroft Foundation,
1, The Green, Bradgate Road,
Anstey, Leicestershire, LE7 7FU,
England.**
or request a copy of our brochure for
more details.

The Foundation will use all donations
to assist those people who are visually
impaired and need special attention
with medical research, diagnosis
and treatment.

Thank you very much for your help.